FAIRY TALES
of IRELAND

W. B. Yeats
FAIRY TALES
of IRELAND

Selected and with an Introduction by
Neil Philip
Illustrated by P. J. Lynch

HarperCollins *Children's Books*

For Roisín

NP

For Katrina

PJL

First published in Great Britain by William Collins Sons & Co Ltd in 1990
This edition published by HarperCollins Children's Books in 2015
HarperCollins Children's Books is a division of HarperCollinsPublishers Ltd,
HarperCollins Publishers
1 London Bridge Street
London SE1 9GF
The HarperCollins Children's Books website address is
www.harpercollins.co.uk

3

978-0-00-794839-0

Printed and bound in England by
Clays Ltd, St Ives plc

Contents

Introduction

1	The Stolen Child	1
2	The Priest's Supper	4
3	The Legend of Knockgrafton	10
4	A Donegal Fairy	17
5	Jamie Freel and the Young Lady	18
6	A Legend of Knockmany	28
7	The Twelve Wild Geese	45
8	The Lazy Beauty and her Aunts	53
9	The Haughty Princess	61
10	Far Darrig in Donegal	66
11	Donald and his Neighbours	71
12	Master and Man	78
13	The Witches' Excursion	87
14	The Man Who Never Knew Fear	91
15	The Horned Women	99
16	Daniel O'Rourke	103
17	The Soul Cages	115
18	The Giant's Stairs	132
19	The Enchantment of Earl Gerald	139
20	The Story of the Little Bird	142
	Notes on the Stories	145

Introduction

The Irish are a nation of talkers, and over the years their talk has run richly and naturally into story. Folk and fairy tales of all kinds abound, from long sagas of legendary heroes to personal accounts of dealings with the fairies, from wonder tales full of magic and transformation to comic anecdotes about local characters, from legends of saints or popular history to shivering ghost stories.

The *Irish Fairy Tales* in this book are chosen from two volumes edited by the Irish poet William Butler Yeats when he was a young man: *Fairy and Folk Tales of the Irish Peasantry* (1888) and *Irish Fairy Tales* (1892). They offer examples of various kinds of story, and various ways of writing down stories which were meant to be heard, not read. But most of all they concentrate on the fairies themselves, creatures which fascinated Yeats, who all his life was entranced by the otherworld. He yearned to know more about these 'Nations of gay creatures, having no souls; nothing in their bright bodies but a mouthful of sweet air.'

On the fourteenth of October, 1892, he was rewarded with a strange experience, which he described in his book *The Celtic Twilight*. Here is his account from a letter written the very next day:

> I went to a great fairy locality – a cave by the Rosses sands – with an uncle & a cousin who is believed by the neighbours & herself to have narrowly escaped capture by that dim kingdom once. I made a magical circle & invoked the fairies. My uncle – a hard headed man of about 47 – heard presently voices like those of boys shouting & distant music but saw nothing. My cousin however saw a bright light & multitudes of little forms clad in crimson as well as hearing the music & then the far voices. Once there was a great sound as of little people cheering & stamping with their feet away in the heart of the rock. The queen of the troop came then – I could see her – & held a long conversation with us & finally wrote in the sand 'be careful & do not seek to know too much about us'.

Others have received much the same warning. Old Biddy Hart told Yeats much about the fairies, but for long she turned his questions aside with, 'I always mind my own affairs, and they always mind theirs.' Another informant, 'Paddy Flynn, a little bright-eyed old man, who lived in a leaky and one-roomed cabin in the village of Ballisodare' answered Yeats's query as to whether he had ever seen the fairies with the long-suffering, 'Am I not annoyed with them?' Yet another, an old Galway countryman renowned as a seer and healer whom Yeats calls Kirwan, told him, 'I see them in all places, and there's no man mowing a meadow that doesn't see them at some time or other.' Yeats's home district in County Sligo was full of such beliefs.

Yeats was born in Dublin in 1865, and died in 1939. He won the Nobel Prize for Literature in 1923, and he was the central figure of the Irish literary revival in the early years of this century. Much of that revival, including the work of Yeats and his close friends Lady Augusta Gregory and John Millington Synge, drew its strength from the rediscovery of traditional story and traditional speech. Yeats's two collections of Irish fairy tales stand at the head of this rediscovery. Indeed he said of *Fairy and Folk Tales* that, 'It was meant for Irish poets. They should draw on it for plots and atmosphere.' He showed he meant what he said in a generous letter to the poet Nora Hopper, who had been accused of stealing from him: 'It has given me great pleasure to find by stray words & sentences that my own little collections of Irish folk lore have been of use to you.'

His own interest in folk traditions was aroused as a young child in visits to his cousin George Middleton at Rosses, County Sligo: 'It was through the Middletons perhaps that I got my interest in country stories, and certainly the first faery-stories that I heard were in cottages about their houses.' His mother and her servant, a fisherman's wife, were good storytellers, too, and in *The Celtic Twilight*, his book of about fairy lore, Yeats published an account of one of their story sessions.

By his early twenties, the poet was already 'searching for people to tell me fairy stories' and noting them down. So the commission from Ernest Rhys (later editor of the 'Everyman' series for J. M. Dent) to compile for the Camelot Series a representative collection of Irish fairy stories was a wonderful opportunity for the young man to explore the published and unpublished treasure trove of Irish story. In a few months of furious work, spurred on equally by enthusiasm for his task and the thought of the seven guineas it would earn him, Yeats ransacked all the available books and journals, and added new material of his own and from the collections of his friend Douglas Hyde.

Douglas Hyde, later the first President of the Republic of Ireland, was immensely helpful to Yeats, who in turn wrote of him, 'Hyde is the best of all the Irish folklorists – His style is perfect – so sincere and simple – so little literary.' The truth of this was proved in 1890 with the publication, through Yeats's intervention, of Hyde's marvellous collection of stories *Beside the Fire*. Later, Hyde was to encourage the work of the Irish Folklore Commission (now the Department of Irish Folklore, University College, Dublin) under the direction of his old assistant James Delargy, which sent collectors to every corner of Ireland in search of stories and traditions, with the result that its archives are now the envy of the world. Its archivist, Seán O'Sullivan, has published two representative collections, *Folktales of Ireland* (1966) and *Legends from Ireland* (1977). These, together with Henry Glassie's *Irish Folk Tales* (1985), give a fair sample of the riches now available to anyone interested in Irish folklore.

But in 1888 when Yeats compiled his *Folk and Fairy Tales,* while there was still a vibrant storytelling tradition in Ireland, very little of it had been written down, and what there was was often spoilt by the writers, who ignored what Lady Gregory called 'the beautiful rhythmic sentences' of the original tellers and put the stories, rued Yeats, into 'newspaper English' on the one hand or 'ramshackle towrow dialect' on the other. So Yeats had to search hard to find stories from early collectors such as Thomas Crofton Croker, Patrick Kennedy and Letitia McClintock suitable for his book. In his long, favourable review, Oscar Wilde commented particularly on Yeats's 'quick instinct in finding out the best and most beautiful things in Irish folk-lore.' Wilde's own father and mother had been pioneer collectors (one of their stories was 'The Horned Women', p. 109), so his good opinion was cheering. Criticisms by other reviewers of the unscientific and rather literary nature of the book did not trouble its editor, who retorted that 'scientific people cannot tell stories', and sighed, 'Oh these folklorists! and what have they done – murder a few innocent fairy tales.'

In fact Yeats and the scientific folklorists were not as far apart as they thought. Both applauded Douglas Hyde as the best of all Irish folklorists; both agreed with Lady Gregory when she wrote that, 'To gather folk-lore one needs, I think, leisure, patience, reverence, and a good memory.' Despite modern recording equipment, this is still true today.

It was with Lady Gregory that Yeats pursued his interest in folklore, collecting tales, legends and folk beliefs on which he wrote six long essays between 1897 and 1902, incorporating some material in *The Celtic Twilight.* The plan was for the two friends to write a 'big book of folk lore' together, but the bulk of the work was Lady Gregory's, and the book, *Visions and Beliefs in the West of Ireland,* came out in her name, with essays and notes by Yeats. Together with Hyde's *Beside the Fire, Visions and Beliefs* is one of the best books on Irish traditions of the era before sound recording. Lady Gregory, like Hyde, had patience and reverence, and also what Yeats called 'the needful subtle imaginative sympathy' to record the tone, the meaning and the context of a story as well as the words in which it is told. She had also, like Hyde mastered Gaelic, the Irish language in which the bulk of Irish stories has been recorded. Without fluent Gaelic, Yeats could never be more than an amateur Irish folklorist.

Still if Yeats was hampered by his English tongue and his educated mind, he loved 'those old rambling moralless tales, which are the delight of the poor and hard-driven wherever life is left in its natural simplicity.' He discerned in such stories as are collected here, 'the simplest and most unforgettable thoughts of the generations', declaring that 'Folk-art . . . is the soil where all great art is rooted.' Yeats was himself a great artist, and he recognised in the melancholy, extravagant, spellbinding narratives of unlettered Irish storytellers a poetry and a passion akin to his own.

Neil Philip, 1989

1: THE STOLEN CHILD

W. B. Yeats

Where dips the rocky highland
    Of Sleuth Wood in the lake,
There lies a leafy island
    Where flapping herons wake
The drowsy water–rats.
There we've hid our fairy vats
Full of berries,
And of reddest stolen cherries.
Come away, O, human child!
To the woods and waters wild
With a fairy hand in hand,
For the world's more full of weeping than
        you can understand.

Where the wave of moonlight glosses
    The dim grey sands with light,
Far off by farthest Rosses
    We foot it all the night,
Weaving olden dances,
Mingling hands, and mingling glances,
    Till the moon has taken flight;

To and fro we leap,
    And chase the frothy bubbles,
    While the world is full of troubles.
And is anxious in its sleep.
Come away! O, human child!
To the woods and waters wild,
With a fairy hand in hand,
For the world's more full of weeping than
        you can understand.

Where the wandering water gushes
    From the hills above Glen–Car,
In pools among the rushes,
    That scarce could bathe a star,
We seek for slumbering trout,
    And whispering in their ears;
      We give them evil dreams,
Leaning softly out
    From ferns that drop their tears
      Of dew on the young streams.
Come! O, human child!
To the woods and waters wild,
With a fairy hand in hand,
For the world's more full of weeping than
        you can understand.

The Stolen Child

Away with us, he's going,
   The solemn-eyed;
He'll hear no more the lowing
   Of the calves on the warm hill-side.
Or the kettle on the hob
   Sing peace into his breast;
Or see the brown mice bob
   Round and round the oatmeal chest.
For he comes, the human child,
To the woods and waters wild,
With a fairy hand in hand,
For the world's more full of weeping than
   he can understand.

2: THE PRIEST'S SUPPER

It is said by those who ought to understand such things, that the good people, or the fairies, are some of the angels who were turned out of heaven, and who landed on their feet in this world, while the rest of their companions, who had more sin to sink them, went down farther to a worse place. Be this as it may, there was a merry troop of the fairies, dancing and playing all manner of wild pranks, on a bright moonlight evening towards the end of September.

The scene of their merriment was not far distant from Inchegeela, in the west of the county Cork – a poor village, although it had a barrack for soldiers; but great mountains and barren rocks, like those round about it, are enough to strike poverty into any place: however as the fairies can have everything they want for wishing, poverty does not trouble them much, and all their care is to seek out unfrequented nooks and places where it is not likely anyone will come to spoil their sport.

On a nice green sod by the river's side were the little fellows dancing in a ring as gaily as may be, with their red caps wagging about at every bound in the moonshine, and so light were these bounds that the lobs of dew, although they trembled under their feet, were not disturbed by their capering. Thus did they carry on their gambols, spinning round and round, and twirling and bobbing and diving, and going through all manner of figures, until

4

one of them chirped out,

> "Cease, cease, with your drumming,
> Here's an end to our mumming;
> By my smell
> I can tell
> A priest this way is coming!"

And away every one of the fairies scampered off as hard as they could, concealing themselves under the green leaves of the foxglove, where, if their little red caps should happen to peep out, they would only look like its crimson bells; and more hid themselves at the shady side of stones and brambles, and others under the bank of the river, and in holes and crannies of one kind or another.

The fairy speaker was not mistaken; for along the road, which was within view of the river, came Father Horrigan on his pony, thinking to himself that as it was so late he would make an end of his journey at the first cabin he came to. According to his determination, he stopped at the dwelling of Dermod Leary, lifted the latch, and entered with "My blessing on all here".

I need not say that Father Horrigan was a welcome guest wherever he went, for no man was more pious or better beloved in the country. Now it was a great trouble to Dermod that he had nothing to offer his reverence for supper as a relish to the potatoes, which "the old woman", for so Dermod called his wife, though she was not much past twenty, had down boiling in a pot over the fire; he thought of the net which he had set in the river, but as it had been there only a short time, the chances were against his finding a fish in it. "No matter," thought Dermod, "there can be no harm in stepping down to try; and maybe, as I want fish for the priest's supper, that one will be there before me."

Down to the river-side went Dermod, and he found in the net as fine a salmon as ever jumped in the bright waters of "the spreading Lee"; but as he was going to take it out, the net was pulled from him, he could not tell how or by whom, and away got the salmon, and went swimming along with the current as gaily as if nothing had happened.

Dermod looked sorrowfully at the wake which the fish had left upon the water, shining like a line of silver in the moonlight, and then, with an angry motion of his right hand, and a stamp of his foot, gave vent to his feelings by muttering, "May bitter bad luck attend you night and day for a blackguard schemer of a salmon, wherever you go! You ought to be ashamed of yourself, if there's any shame in you, to give me the slip after this fashion! And I'm clear in my own mind you'll come to no good, for some kind of evil thing or other helped you – did I not feel it pull the net against me as strong as the devil himself?"

"That's not true for you," said one of the little fairies who had scampered off at the approach of the priest, coming up to Dermod Leary with a whole throng of companions at his heels; "there was only a dozen and a half of us pulling against you."

Dermod gazed on the tiny speaker with wonder, who continued, "Make yourself noways uneasy about the priest's supper; for if you will go back and ask him one question from us, there will be as fine a supper as ever was put on a table spread out before him in less than no time."

"I'll have nothing at all to do with you," replied Dermod in a tone of determination; and after a pause he added, "I'm much obliged to you for your offer, sir, but I know better than to sell myself to you, or the like of you, for a supper; and more than that; I know Father Horrigan has more regard for my soul than to wish me to pledge it for ever, out of regard to anything you could put before him – so there's an end of the matter."

The little speaker, with a pertinacity not to be repulsed by Dermod's manner, continued, "Will you ask the priest one civil question for us?"

Dermod considered for some time, and he was right in doing

so, but he thought that no one could come to harm out of asking a civil question. "I see no objection to do that same, gentlemen," said Dermod; "but I will have nothing in life to do with your supper – mind that."

"Then," said the little speaking fairy, whilst the rest came crowding after him from all parts, "go and ask Father Horrigan to tell us whether our souls will be saved at the last day, like the souls of good Christians; and if you wish us well, bring back word what he says without delay."

Away went Dermod to his cabin, where he found the potatoes thrown out on the table, and his good woman handing the biggest of them all, a beautiful laughing red apple, smoking like a hard-ridden horse on a frosty night, over to Father Horrigan.

"Please your reverence," said Dermod, after some hesitation, "may I make bold to ask your honour one question?"

"What may that be?" said Father Horrigan.

"Why, then, begging your reverence's pardon for my free-dom, it is, if the souls of the good people are to be saved at the last day?"

"Who bid you ask me that question, Leary?" said the priest, fixing his eyes upon him very sternly, which Dermod could not stand before at all.

"I'll tell no lies about the matter, and nothing in life but the truth," said Dermod. "It was the good people themselves who sent me to ask the question, and there they are in thousands down on the bank of the river, waiting for me to go back with the answer."

"Go back by all means," said the priest, "and tell them, if they want to know, to come here to me themselves, and I'll answer that or any other question they are pleased to ask with the greatest pleasure in life."

Dermod accordingly returned to the fairies, who came swarm-ing round about him to hear what the priest had said in reply;

8

and Dermod spoke out among them like a bold man as he was: but when they heard that they must go to the priest, away they fled, some here and more there, and some this way and more that, whisking by poor Dermod so fast and in such numbers that he was quite bewildered.

When he came to himself, which was not for a long time, back he went to his cabin, and ate his dry potatoes along with Father Horrigan, who made quite light of the thing; but Dermod could not help thinking it a mighty hard case that his reverence, whose words had the power to banish the fairies at such a rate, should have no sort of relish to his supper, and that the fine salmon he had in the net should have been got away from him in such a manner.

3: THE LEGEND OF KNOCKGRAFTON

There was once a poor man who lived in the fertile glen of Aherlow, at the foot of the gloomy Galtee mountains, and he had a great hump on his back: he looked just as if his body had been rolled up and placed upon his shoulders; and his head was pressed down with the weight so much that his chin, when he was sitting, used to rest upon his knees for support. The country people were rather shy of meeting him in any lonesome place, for though, poor creature, he was as harmless and as inoffensive as a new-born infant, yet his deformity was so great that he scarcely appeared to be a human creature, and some ill-minded persons had set strange stories about him afloat. He was said to have a great knowledge of herbs and charms; but certain it was that he had a mighty skilful hand in plaiting straws and rushes into hats and baskets, which was the way he made his livelihood.

Lusmore, for that was the nickname put upon him by reason of his always wearing a sprig of the fairy cap, or lusmore (the foxglove), in his little straw hat, would ever get a higher penny for his plaited work than anyone else and perhaps that was the reason why someone, out of envy, had circulated the strange stories about him. Be that as it may, it happened that he was returning one evening from the pretty town of Cahir towards Cappagh, and as little Lusmore walked very slowly, on account of

10

the great hump upon his back, it was quite dark when he came to the old moat of Knockgrafton, which stood on the right-hand side of his road. Tired and weary was he, and noways comfortable in his own mind at thinking how much farther he had to travel, and that he should be walking all the night; so he sat down under the moat to rest himself, and began looking mournfully enough upon the moon, which —

"Rising in clouded majesty, at length
 Apparent Queen, unveil'd her peerless light,
And o'er the dark her silver mantle threw,
 And in her pale dominion check'd the night."

Presently there rose a wild strain of unearthly melody upon the ear of little Lusmore; he listened, and he thought that he had never heard such ravishing music before. It was like the sound of many voices, each mingling and blending with the other so strangely that they seemed to be one, though all singing different strains, and the words of the song were these —

Da Luan, Da Mort, Da Luan, Da Mort, Da Luan, Da Mort;
when there would be a moment's pause, and then the round of melody went on again.

Lusmore listened attentively, scarcely drawing his breath lest he might lose the slightest note. He now plainly perceived that the singing was within the moat; and though at first it had charmed him so much, he began to get tired of hearing the same sound sung over and over so often without any change; so availing himself of the pause when *Da Luan, Da Mort,* had been sung three times, he took up the tune, and raised it with the words *augus Da Cadine* (and Wednesday), and then went on singing with the voices inside of the moat, *Da Luan, Da Mort,* finishing the melody, when the pause again came, with *augus Da Cadine.*

The fairies within Knockgrafton, for the song was a fairy melody, when they heard this addition to the tune, were so much delighted that, with instant resolve, it was determined to

bring the mortal among them, whose musical skill so far exceeded theirs, and little Lusmore was conveyed into their company with the eddying speed of a whirlwind.

Glorious to behold was the sight that burst upon him as he came down through the moat, twirling round and round, with the lightness of a straw, to the sweetest music that kept time to his motion. The greatest honour was then paid him, for he was put above all the musicians, and he had servants tending upon him, and everything to his heart's content, and a hearty welcome to all; and, in short, he was made as much of as if he had been the first man in the land.

Presently Lusmore saw a great consultation going forward among the fairies, and, notwithstanding all their civility, he felt very much frightened, until one stepping out from the rest came up to him and said —

"Lusmore! Lusmore!
Doubt not, nor deplore,
For the hump which you bore
On your back is no more;
Look down on the floor,
And view it, Lusmore!"

When these words were said, poor little Lusmore felt himself so light, and so happy, that he thought he could have bounded at one jump over the moon, like the cow in the history of the cat and the fiddle; and he saw, with inexpressible pleasure, his hump tumble down upon the ground from his shoulders. He then tried to lift up his head, and he did so with becoming caution, fearing that he might knock it against the ceiling of the grand hall, where he was; he looked round and round again with the greatest wonder and delight upon everything, which appeared more and more beautiful; and, overpowered at beholding such a resplendent scene, his head grew dizzy, and his eyesight became dim.

At last he fell into a sound sleep, and when he awoke he found it was broad daylight, the sun shining brightly, and the birds singing sweetly; and that he was lying just at the foot of the moat of Knockgrafton, with the cows and sheep grazing peaceably round about him. The first thing Lusmore did, after saying his prayers, was to put his hand behind to feel for his hump, but no sign of one was there on his back, and he looked at himself with great pride, for he had now become a well-shaped dapper little fellow, and more than that, found himself in a full suit of new clothes, which he concluded the fairies had made for him.

Towards Cappagh he went, stepping out as lightly, and springing up at every step as if he had been all his life a dancing-master. Not a creature who met Lusmore knew him without his hump, and he had a great work to persuade everyone that he was the same man — in truth he was not, so far as the outward appearance went.

Of course it was not long before the story of Lusmore's hump got about, and a great wonder was made of it. Through the country, for miles round, it was the talk of everyone high and low.

One morning, as Lusmore was sitting contented enough at his cabin door, up came an old woman to him, and asked him if he could direct her to Cappagh.

"I need give you no directions, my good woman," said Lusmore, "for this is Cappagh; and whom may you want here?"

"I have come," said the woman, "out of Decie's country, in the county of Waterford, looking after one Lusmore, who, I have heard tell, had his hump taken off by the fairies; for there is a son of a gossip of mine who has got a hump on him that will be his death; and maybe, if he could use the same charm as Lusmore, the hump may be taken off him. And now I have told you the reason of my coming so far: 'tis to find out about this charm, if I can."

Lusmore, who was ever a good-natured little fellow, told the woman all the particulars, how he had raised the tune for the fairies at Knockgrafton, how his hump had been removed from his shoulders, and how he had got a new suit of clothes into the bargain.

The woman thanked him very much, and then went away quite happy and easy in her mind. When she came back to her gossip's house, in the county of Waterford, she told her everything that Lusmore had said, and they put the little hump-backed man, who was a peevish and cunning creature from his birth, upon a cart, and took him all the way across the country. It was a long journey, but they did not care for that, if the hump was taken from off him; and they brought him, just at nightfall, and left him under the old moat of Knockgrafton.

Jack Madden, for that was the humpy man's name, had not been sitting there long when he heard the tune going on within the moat much sweeter than before; for the fairies were singing it the way Lusmore had settled their music for them, and the song was going on: *Da Luan, Da Mort, Da Luan, Da Mort, Da Luan, Da Mort, augus Da Dardeen,* without ever stopping. Jack Madden, who was in a great hurry to get quit of his hump, never thought of waiting until the fairies had done, or watching for a fit opportunity to raise the tune higher again than Lusmore had; so having heard them sing it over seven times without stopping, out he bawls, never minding the time or the humour of the tune, or how he could bring his words in properly, *augus Da Dardeen, augus Da Hena* (and Thursday and Friday), thinking that if one day was good two were better; and that if Lusmore had one new suit of clothes given him, he should have two.

No sooner had the words passed his lips than he was taken up and whisked into the moat with prodigious force; and the fairies came crowding round him with great anger, screeching and screaming, and roaring out, "Who spoiled our tune? who spoiled our tune?" and one stepped up to him above all the rest, and said —

15

"Jack Madden! Jack Madden!
Your words came so bad in
The tune we felt glad in; –
This castle you're had in,
That your life we may sadden;
Here's two humps for Jack Madden!"

And twenty of the strongest fairies brought Lusmore's hump, and put it down upon poor Jack's back, over his own, where it became fixed as firmly as if it was nailed on with twelve-penny nails, by the best carpenter that ever drove one. Out of their castle they then kicked him; and in the morning, when Jack Madden's mother and her gossip came to look after their little man, they found him half dead, lying at the foot of the moat, with the other hump upon his back.

Well to be sure, how they did look at each other! but they were afraid to say anything, lest a hump might be put upon their own shoulders. Home they brought the unlucky Jack Madden with them, as downcast in their hearts and their looks as ever two gossips were; and what through the weight of his other hump, and the long journey, he died soon after, leaving, they say, his heavy curse to anyone who would go to listen to fairy tunes again.

4: A DONEGAL FAIRY

Ay, it's a bad thing to displeasure the gentry, sure enough — they can be unfriendly if they're angered, an' they can be the very best o' gude neighbours if they're treated kindly.

My mother's sister was her lone in the house one day, wi' a big pot o' water boiling on the fire, and ane o' the wee folk fell down the chimney, and slipped wi' his leg in the hot water.

He let a terrible squeal out o' him, an' in a minute the house was full o' wee creatures pulling him out o' the pot, an' carrying him across the floor.

"Did she scald you?" my aunt heard them saying to him.

"Na, na, it was mysel' scalded my ainsel'," quoth the wee fellow.

"A weel, a weel," says they. "If it was your ainsel scalded yoursel', we'll say nothing; but if she had scalded you, we'd ha' made her pay."

5: JAMIE FREEL AND THE YOUNG LADY

Down in Fannet, in times gone by, lived Jamie Freel and his mother. Jamie was the widow's sole support; his strong arm worked for her untiringly, and as each Saturday night came round, he poured his wages into her lap, thanking her dutifully for the halfpence which she returned him for tobacco.

He was extolled by his neighbours as the best son ever known or heard of. But he had neighbours, of whose opinion he was ignorant – neighbours who lived pretty close to him, whom he had never seen, who are, indeed, rarely seen by mortals, except on May eves and Halloweens.

An old ruined castle, about a quarter of a mile from his cabin, was said to be the abode of the "wee folk". Every Halloween were the ancient windows lighted up, and passers-by saw little figures flitting to and fro inside the building, while they heard the music of pipes and flutes.

It was well known that fairy revels took place; but nobody had the courage to intrude on them.

Jamie had often watched the little figures from a distance, and listened to the charming music, wondering what the inside of the castle was like; but one Halloween he got up and took his cap, saying to his mother, "I'm awa' to the castle to seek my fortune."

"What!" cried she, "would you venture there? you that's the

poor widow's one son! Dinna be sae venturesome an' folitch, Jamie! They'll kill you, an' then what'll come o' me?"

"Never fear, mother; nae harm 'ill happen me, but I maun gae."

He set out, and as he crossed the potato field, came in sight of the castle, whose windows were ablaze with light, that seemed to turn the russet leaves, still clinging to the crabtree branches, into gold.

Halting in the grove at one side of the ruin, he listened to the elfin revelry, and the laughter and singing made him all the more determined to proceed.

Numbers of little people, the largest about the size of a child of five years old, were dancing to the music of flutes and fiddles, while others drank and feasted.

"Welcome, Jamie Freel! welcome, welcome, Jamie!" cried the company, perceiving their visitor. The word "Welcome" was caught up and repeated by every voice in the castle.

Time flew, and Jamie was enjoying himself very much, when his hosts said, "We're going to ride to Dublin tonight to steal a young lady. Will you come too, Jamie Freel?"

"Aye, that will I!" cried the rash youth, thirsting for adventure.

A troop of horses stood at the door. Jamie mounted and his steed rose with him into the air. He was presently flying over his mother's cottage, surrounded by the elfin troop, and on and on they went, over bold mountains, over little hills, over the deep Lough Swilley, over towns and cottages, where people were burning nuts, and eating apples, and keeping merry Halloween. It seemed to Jamie that they flew all round Ireland before they got to Dublin.

"This is Derry," said the fairies, flying over the cathedral spire; and what was said by one voice was repeated by all the rest, till fifty little voices were crying out, "Derry! Derry! Derry!"

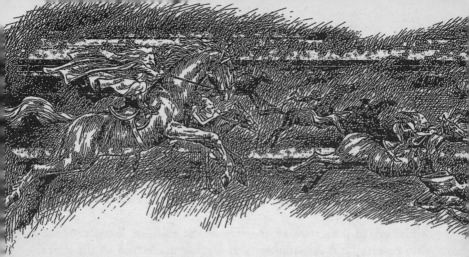

In like manner was Jamie informed as they passed over each town on the route, and at length he heard the silvery voices cry, "Dublin! Dublin!"

It was no mean dwelling that was to be honoured by the fairy visit, but one of the finest houses in Stephen's Green.

The troop dismounted near a window, and Jamie saw a beautiful face, on a pillow in a splendid bed. He saw the young lady lifted and carried away, while the stick which was dropped in her place on the bed took her exact form.

The lady was placed before one rider and carried a short way, then given to another, and the names of the towns were cried out as before.

They were approaching home. Jamie heard "Rathmullan", "Milford", "Tamney", and then he knew they were near his own house.

"You've all had your turn at carrying the young lady," said he. "Why wouldn't I get her for a wee piece?"

"Ay, Jamie," replied they, pleasantly, "you may take your turn at carrying her, to be sure."

Holding his prize very tightly, he dropped down near his mother's door.

"Jamie Freel, Jamie Freel! is that the way you treat us?" cried they, and they too dropped down near the door.

Jamie held fast, though he knew not what he was holding, for the little folk turned the lady into all sorts of strange shapes. At one moment she was a black dog, barking and trying to bite; at another, a glowing bar of iron, which yet had no heat; then, again, a sack of wool.

But still Jamie held her, and the baffled elves were turning away, when a tiny woman, the smallest of the party, exclaimed, "Jamie Freel has her awa' frae us, but he sall hae nae gude o' her, for I'll mak' her deaf and dumb," and she threw something over the young girl.

While they rode off disappointed, Jamie lifted the latch and went in.

"Jamie, man!" cried his mother, "you've been awa' all night; what have they done on you?"

"Naething bad, mother; I ha' the very best of gude luck. Here's a beautiful young lady I ha' brought you for company."

"Bless us an' save us!" exclaimed the mother, and for some minutes she was so astonished that she could not think of anything else to say.

Jamie told his story of the night's adventure, ending by saying, "Surely you wouldna have allowed me to let her gang with them to be lost forever?"

"But a *lady*, Jamie! How can a lady eat we'er poor diet, and live in we'er poor way? I ax you that, you foolitch fellow?"

"Weel, mother, sure it's better for her to be here nor over yonder," and he pointed in the direction of the castle.

Meanwhile, the deaf and dumb girl shivered in her light clothing, stepping close to the humble turf fire.

"Poor creature, she's quare and handsome! Nae wonder they set their hearts on her," said the old woman, gazing at her guest with pity and admiration. "We maun dress her first; but what, in the name o' fortune, hae I fit for the likes o' her to wear?"

She went to her press in "the room", and took out her Sunday gown of brown drugget; she then opened a drawer and drew forth a pair of white stockings, a long snowy garment of fine linen, and a cap, her "dead dress", as she called it.

These articles of attire had long been ready for a certain triste ceremony, in which she would some day fill the chief part, and only saw the light occasionally, when they were hung out to air; but she was willing to give even these to the fair trembling visitor, who was turning in dumb sorrow and wonder from her to Jamie, and from Jamie back to her.

The poor girl suffered herself to be dressed, and then sat down on a "creepie" in the chimney corner, and buried her face in her hands.

"What'll we do to keep up a lady like thou?" cried the old woman.

"I'll work for you both, mother," replied the son.

"An' how could a lady live on we'er poor diet?" she repeated.

"I'll work for her," was all Jamie's answer.

He kept his word. The young lady was very sad for a long time, and tears stole down her cheeks many an evening while the old woman spun by the fire, and Jamie made salmon nets, an accomplishment lately acquired by him, in hopes of adding to the comfort of his guest.

But she was always gentle, and tried to smile when she perceived them looking at her; and by degrees she adapted herself to their ways and mode of life. It was not very long before she began to feed the pig, mash potatoes and meal for the fowls, and knit blue worsted socks.

So a year passed, and Halloween came round again. "Mother," said Jamie, taking down his cap, "I'm off to the ould castle to seek my fortune."

"Are you mad, Jamie?" cried his mother, in terror; "sure they'll kill you this time for what you done on them last year."

Jamie made light of her fears and went his way.

As he reached the crabtree grove, he saw bright lights in the castle windows as before, and heard loud talking. Creeping under the window, he heard the wee folk say, "That was a poor trick Jamie Freel played us this night last year, when he stole the nice young lady from us."

"Ay," said the tiny woman, "an' I punished him for it, for there she sits, a dumb image by his hearth; but he does na' know that three drops out o' this glass I hold in my hand wad gie her her hearing and her speeches back again."

Jamie's heart beat fast as he entered the hall. Again he was greeted by a chorus of welcomes from the company — "Here comes Jamie Freel! welcome, welcome, Jamie!"

As soon as the tumult subsided, the little woman said, "You be to drink our health, Jamie, out o' this glass in my hand."

Jamie snatched the glass from her and darted to the door. He never knew how he reached his cabin, but he arrived there breathless, and sank on a stove by the fire.

"You're kilt surely this time, my poor boy," said his mother.

"No, indeed, better luck than ever this time!" and he gave the lady three drops of the liquid that still remained at the bottom of the glass, notwithstanding his mad race over the potato field.

The lady began to speak, and her first words were words of thanks to Jamie.

The three inmates of the cabin had so much to say to one another, that long after cock-crow, when the fairy music had quite ceased, they were talking round the fire.

"Jamie," said the lady, "be pleased to get me paper and pen and ink, that I may write to my father, and tell him what has become of me."

She wrote, but weeks passed, and she received no answer. Again and again she wrote, and still no answer.

At length she said, "You must come with me to Dublin, Jamie, to find my father."

"I ha' no money to hire a cart for you," he replied, "an' how can you travel to Dublin on your foot?"

But she implored him so much that he consented to set out with her, and walk all the way from Fannet to Dublin. It was not as easy as the fairy journey; but at last they rang the bell at the door of the house in Stephen's Green.

"Tell my father that his daughter is here," said she to the servant who opened the door.

"The gentleman that lives here has no daughter, my girl. He had one, but she died better nor a year ago."

"Do you not know me, Sullivan?"

"No, poor girl, I do not."

"Let me see the gentleman. I only ask to see him."

"Well, that's not much to ax; we'll see what can be done."

In a few moments the lady's father came to the door.

"Dear Father," said she, "don't you know me?"

"How dare you call me Father?" cried the old gentleman, angrily. "You are an imposter. I have no daughter."

"Look in my face, Father, and surely you'll remember me."

"My daughter is dead and buried. She died a long, long time ago." The old gentleman's voice changed from anger to sorrow. "You can go," he concluded.

"Stop, dear Father, till you look at this ring on my finger. Look at your name and mine engraved on it."

"It certainly is my daughter's ring; but I do not know how you came by it. I fear in no honest way."

"Call my mother, *she* will be sure to know me," said the poor girl, who, by this time, was crying bitterly.

"My poor wife is beginning to forget her sorrow. She seldom speaks of her daughter now. Why should I renew her grief by reminding her of her loss?"

But the young lady persevered, till at last the mother was sent for.

"Mother," she began, when the old lady came to the door, "don't *you* know your daughter?"

"I have no daughter; my daughter died and was buried a long, long time ago."

"Only look in my face, and surely you'll know me."

The old lady shook her head.

"You have all forgotten me; but look at this mole on my neck. Surely, Mother, you know me now?"

"Yes, yes," said the mother, "my Gracie had a mole on her neck like that; but then I saw her in her coffin, and saw the lid shut down upon her."

It became Jamie's turn to speak, and he gave the history of the fairy journey, of the theft of the young lady, of the figure he had seen laid in its place, of her life with his mother in Fannet, of last Halloween, and of the three drops that had released her from her enchantment.

She took up the story when he paused, and told how kind the mother and son had been to her.

The parents could not make enough of Jamie. They treated him with every distinction, and when he expressed his wish to return to Fannet, said they did not know what to do to show their gratitude.

But an awkward complication arose. The daughter would not let him go without her. "If Jamie goes, I'll go too," she said. "He saved me from the fairies, and has worked for me ever since. If it had not been for him, dear Father and Mother, you would never have seen me again. If he goes, I'll go too."

This being her resolution, the old gentleman said that Jamie should become his son-in-law. The mother was brought from Fannet in a coach and four, and there was a splendid wedding.

They all lived together in the grand Dublin house, and Jamie was heir to untold wealth at his father-in-law's death.

6: A LEGEND OF KNOCKMANY

What Irish man, woman, or child has not heard of our renowned Hibernian Hercules, the great and glorious Fin M'Coul? Not one, from Cape Clear to the Giant's Causeway, nor from that back again to Cape Clear. And, by the way, speaking of the Giant's Causeway brings me at once to the beginning of my story.

Well, it so happened that Fin and his gigantic relatives were all working at the Causeway, in order to make a bridge, or what was still better, a good stout pad-road, across to Scotland; when Fin, who was very fond of his wife Oonagh, took it into his head that he would go home and see how the poor woman got on in his absence. To be sure, Fin was a true Irishman, and so the sorrow thing in life brought him back, only to see that she was snug and comfortable, and, above all things, that she got her rest well at night; for he knew that the poor woman, when he was with her, used to be subject to nightly qualms and configurations, that kept him very anxious, decent man, striving to keep her up to the good spirits and health that she had when they were first married. So, accordingly, he pulled up a fir tree, and, after lopping off the roots and branches, made a walking stick of it, and set out on his way to Oonagh.

Oonagh, or rather Fin, lived at this time on the very tip-top of Knockmany Hill, which faces a cousin of its own called Cullamore, that rises up, half-hill, half-mountain, on the opposite side – east-east by south, as the sailors say, when they wish to puzzle a landsman.

Now, the truth is, for it must come out, that honest Fin's affection for his wife, though cordial enough in itself, was by no manner of means the real cause of his journey home. There was at that time another giant, named Cucullin – some say he was Irish, and some say he was Scotch – but whether Scotch or Irish, sorrow doubt of it but he was a *targer*. No other giant of the day could stand before him; and such was his strength, that, when well vexed, he could give a stamp that shook the country about him. The fame and name of him went far and near; and nothing in the shape of a man, it was said, had any chance with him in a fight. Whether the story is true or not, I cannot say, but the report went that, by one blow of his fists he flattened a thunderbolt, and kept it in his pocket, in the shape of a pancake, to show to all his enemies, when they were about to fight him.

Undoubtedly he had given every giant in Ireland a considerable beating, barring Fin M'Coul himself; and he swore, by the solemn contents of Moll Kelly's Primer, that he would never rest, night or day, winter or summer, till he would serve Fin with the same sauce, if he could catch him. Fin, however, who no doubt was the cock of the walk on his own dunghill, had a strong disinclination to meet a giant who could make a young earthquake, or flatten a thunderbolt when he was angry; so accordingly kept dodging about from place to place, not much to his credit as a Trojan, to be sure, whenever he happened to get the hard word that Cucullin was on the scent of him. This, then, was the marrow of the whole movement, although he put it on his anxiety to see Oonagh; and I am not saying but there was some truth in that too.

However, the short and long of it was, with reverence be it spoken, that he heard Cucullin was coming to the Causeway to

have a trial of strength with him; and he was naturally enough seized, in consequence, with a very warm and sudden fit of affection for his wife, poor woman, who was delicate in her health, and leading, besides, a very lonely, uncomfortable life of it (he assured them) in his absence. He accordingly pulled up the fir tree, as I said before, and having *snedded* it into a walking stick, set out on his affectionate travels to see his darling Oonagh on the top of Knockmany, by the way.

In truth, to state the suspicions of the country at the time, the people wondered very much why it was that Fin selected such a windy spot for his dwelling-house, and they even went so far as to tell him as much.

"What can you mane, Mr M'Coul," said they, "by pitching your tent upon the top of Knockmany, where you never are without a breeze, day or night, winter or summer, and where you're often forced to take your nightcap* without either going to bed or turning up your little finger; ay, an' where, besides this, there's the sorrow's own want of water?"

"Why," said Fin, "ever since I was the height of a round

*A common name for the cloud or rack that hangs, as a forerunner of wet weather, about the peak of a mountain.

tower, I was known to be fond of having a good prospect of my own; and where the dickens, neighbours, could I find a better spot for a good prospect than the top of Knockmany? As for water, I am sinking a pump,† and, plase goodness, as soon as the Causeway's made, I intend to finish it."

Now, this was more of Fin's philosophy; for the real state of the case was, that he pitched upon the top of Knockmany in order that he might be able to see Cucullin coming towards the house, and, of course, that he himself might go to look after his distant transactions in other parts of the country, rather than — but no matter — we do not wish to be too hard on Fin. All we have to say is, that if he wanted a spot from which to keep a sharp look-out — and, between ourselves, he did want it grievously — barring Slieve Croob, or Slieve Donard, or its own cousin, Cullamore, he could not find a neater or more convenient situation for it in the sweet and sagacious province of Ulster.

"God save all here!" said Fin, good-humouredly, on putting his honest face into his own door.

"Musha, Fin, avick, an' you're welcome home to your own Oonagh, you darlin' bully." Here followed a smack that is said to have made the waters of the lake at the bottom of the hill curl, as it were, with kindness and sympathy.

"Faith," said Fin, "beautiful; an' how are you, Oonagh — and how did you sport your figure during my absence, my bilberry?"

"Never a merrier — as bouncing a grass widow as ever there was in sweet 'Tyrone among the bushes'."

Fin gave a short, good-humoured cough, and laughed most heartily, to show her how much he was delighted that she made herself happy in his absence.

"An' what brought you home so soon, Fin?" said she.

"Why, avourneen," said Fin, putting in his answer in the proper way, "never the thing but the purest of love and affection

† There is upon the top of this hill an opening that bears a very strong resemblance to the crater of an extinct volcano.

for yourself. Sure you know that truth, anyhow, Oonagh."

Fin spent two or three happy days with Oonagh, and felt himself very comfortable, considering the dread he had of Cucullin. This, however, grew upon him so much that his wife could not but perceive something lay on his mind which he kept altogether to himself. Let a woman alone, in the meantime, for ferreting, or wheedling a secret out of her good man, when she wishes. Fin was a proof of this.

"It's this Cucullin," said he, "that's troubling me. When the fellow gets angry, and begins to stamp, he'll shake you a whole townland; and it's well known that he can stop a thunderbolt, for he always carries one about him in the shape of a pancake, to show to anyone that might misdoubt it."

As he spoke, he clapped his thumb in his mouth, which he always did when he wanted to prophesy, or to know anything that happened in his absence; and the wife, who knew what he did it for, said, very sweetly,

"Fin, darling, I hope you don't bite your thumb at me, dear?"

"No," said Fin; "but I bite my thumb, acushla," said he.

"Yes, jewel; but take care and don't draw blood," said she. "Ah, Fin! don't, my bully – don't."

"He's coming," said Fin; "I see him below Dungannon."

"Thank goodness, dear! an' who is it, avick? Glory be to God!"

"That baste, Cucullin," replied Fin; "and how to manage I don't know. If I run away, I am disgraced; and I know that sooner or later I must meet him, for my thumb tells me so."

"When will he be here?" said she.

"Tomorrow, about two o'clock," replied Fin, with a groan.

"Well, my bully, don't be cast down," said Oonagh; "depend on me, and maybe I'll bring you better out of this scrape than ever you could bring yourself, by your rule o' thumb."

This quieted Fin's heart very much, for he knew that Oonagh was hand and glove with the fairies; and, indeed, to tell the truth, she was supposed to be a fairy herself. If she was, however, she must have been a kind-hearted one, for, by all accounts, she never did anything but good in the neighbourhood.

Now it so happened that Oonagh had a sister named Granua, living opposite them, on the very top of Cullamore, which I have mentioned already, and this Granua was quite as powerful as herself. The beautiful valley that lies between them is not more than about three or four miles broad, so that of a summer's evening, Granua and Oonagh were able to hold many an agreeable conversation across it, from the one hill-top to the other. Upon this occasion Oonagh resolved to consult her sister as to what was best to be done in the difficulty that surrounded them.

"Granua," said she, "are you at home?"

"No," said the other; "I'm picking bilberries in Althadhawan" (the Devil's Glen).

"Well," said Oonagh, "get up to the top of Cullamore, look about you, and then tell us what you see."

"Very well," replied Granua; after a few minutes, "I am there now."

"What do you see?" asked the other.

"Goodness be about us!" exclaimed Granua, "I see the biggest giant that ever was known coming up from Dungannon."

"Ay," said Oonagh, "that's our difficulty. That giant is the great Cucullin; and he's now commin' up to leather Fin. What's to be done?"

"I'll call to him," she replied, "to come up to Cullamore and refresh himself, and maybe that will give you and Fin time to think of some plan to get yourselves out of the scrape. But," she proceeded, "I'm short of butter, having in the house only half-a-dozen firkins, and as I'm to have a few giants and giantesses to spend the evenin' with me, I'd feel thankful, Oonagh, if you'd throw me up fifteen or sixteen tubs, or the largest churn you have got, and you'll oblige me very much."

"I'll do that with a heart and a half," replied Oonagh; "and, indeed, Granua, I feel myself under great obligations to you for your kindness in keeping him off of us till we see what can be done; for what would become of us all if anything happened to Fin, poor man."

She accordingly got the largest churn of butter she had — which might be about the weight of a couple a dozen mill-stones, so that you may easily judge of its size — and calling up to her sister, "Granua," said she, "are you ready? I'm going to throw you up a churn, so be prepared to catch it."

"I will," said the other; "a good throw now, and take care it does not fall short."

Oonagh threw it; but in consequence of her anxiety about Fin and Cucullin, she forgot to say the charm that was to send it up, so that, instead of reaching Cullamore, as she expected, it fell about half-way between the two hills, at the edge of the Broad Bog near Augher.

"My curse upon you!" she exclaimed; "you've disgraced me. I now change you into a grey stone. Lie there as a testimony of what has happened; and may evil betide the first living man that will ever attempt to remove or injure you!"

And, sure enough, there it lies to this day, with the mark of the four fingers and thumb imprinted in it, exactly as it came out of her hand.

"Never mind," said Granua, "I must only do the best I can with Cucullin. If all fail, I'll give him a cast of heather broth to keep the wind out of his stomach, or panada of oak-bark to draw it in a bit; but, above all things, think of some plan to get Fin out of the scrape he's in, otherwise he's a lost man. You know you used to be sharp and ready-witted; and my own opinion, Oonagh, is, that it will go hard with you, or you'll outdo Cucullin yet."

She then made a high smoke on the top of the hill, after which she put her finger in her mouth, and gave three whistles, and by that Cucullin knew he was invited to Cullamore – for this was the way that the Irish long ago gave a sign to all strangers and travellers, to let them know they were welcome to come and take share of whatever was going.

In the meantime, Fin was very melancholy, and did not know what to do, or how to act at all. Cucullin was an ugly customer, no doubt, to meet with; and, moreover, the idea of the confounded "cake" aforesaid flattened the very heart within him. What chance could he have, strong and brave though he was, with a man who could, when put in a passion, walk the country into earthquakes and knock thunderbolts into pancakes? The thing was impossible; and Fin knew not on what hand to turn him. Right or left – backward or forward – where to go he could form no guess whatsoever.

"Oonagh," said he, "can you do nothing for me? Where's all your invention? Am I to be skivered like a rabbit before your eyes, and to have my name disgraced forever in the sight of all my tribe, and me the best man among them? How am I to fight this man-mountain – this huge cross between an earthquake and a thunderbolt? – with a pancake in his pocket that was once –"

"Be easy Fin," replied Oonagh; "troth, I'm ashamed of you. Keep your toe in your pump, will you? Talking of pancakes,

35

maybe we'll give him as good as any he brings with him — thunderbolt or otherwise. If I don't treat him to as smart feeding as he's got this many a day, never trust Oonagh again. Leave him to me, and do just as I bid you."

This relieved Fin very much; for, after all, he had great confidence in his wife, knowing, as he did, that she had got him out of many a quandary before. The present, however, was the greatest of all; but still he began to get courage, and was able to eat his victuals as usual. Oonagh then drew the nine woollen threads of different colours, which she always did to find out the best way of succeeding in anything of importance she went about. She then platted them into three plats with three colours in each, putting one on her right arm, one round her heart, and the third round her right ankle, for then she knew that nothing could fail with her that she undertook.

Having everything prepared, she sent round to the neighbours and borrowed one-and-twenty iron griddles, which she took and kneaded into the hearts of one-and-twenty cakes of bread, and these she baked on the fire in the usual way, setting them aside in the cupboard according as they were done. She then put down a large pot of new milk, which she made into curds and whey, and gave Fin due instructions how to use the curds when Cucullin should come. Having done all this, she sat down quite contented, waiting for his arrival on the next day about two o'clock, that being the hour at which he was expected — for Fin knew as much by the sucking of his thumb.

Now, this was a curious property that Fin's thumb had; but, notwithstanding all the wisdom and logic he used, to suck out of it, it could never have stood to him here were it not for the wit of his wife. In this very thing, moreover, he was very much resembled by his great foe, Cucullin; for it was well known that the huge strength he possessed all lay in the middle finger of his right hand, and that, if he happened by any mischance to lose it,

he was no more, notwithstanding his bulk, than a common man.

At length, the next day, he was seen coming across the valley, and Oonagh knew that it was time to commence operations. She immediately made the cradle, and desired Fin to lie down in it, and cover himself up with the clothes.

"You must pass for your own child," said she; "so just lie there snug, and say nothing, but be guided by me." This, to be sure, was wormwood to Fin – I mean going into the cradle in such a cowardly manner – but he knew Oonagh well; and finding that he had nothing else for it, with a very rueful face he gathered himself into it, and lay snug, as she had desired him.

About two o'clock, as he had been expected, Cucullin came in. "God save all here!" said he; "is this where the great Fin M'Coul lives?"

"Indeed it is, honest man," replied Oonagh; "God save you kindly – won't you be sitting?"

"Thank you, ma'am," says he, sitting down; "you're Mrs M'Coul, I suppose?"

"I am," said she; "and I have no reason, I hope, to be ashamed of my husband."

"No," said the other, "he has the name of being the strongest and bravest man in Ireland; but for all that, there's a man not far from you that's very desirous of taking a shake with him. Is he at home?"

"Why, then, no," she replied; "and if ever a man left his house in a fury, he did. It appears that someone told him of a big basthoon of a giant called Cucullin being down at the Causeway to look for him, and so he set out there to try if he could catch him. Troth, I hope, for the poor giant's sake, he won't meet him, for if he does, Fin will make paste of him at once."

"Well," said the other, "I am Cucullin, and I have been seeking him these twelve months, but he always kept clear of me; and I will never rest night or day till I lay my hands on him."

At this Oonagh set up a loud laugh, of great contempt, by the way, and looked at him as if he was only a mere handful of a man.

"Did you ever see Fin?" said she, changing her manner all at once.

"How could I?" said he; "he always took care to keep his distance."

"I thought so," she replied; "I judged as much; and if you take my advice, you poor-looking creature, you'll pray night and day that you may never see him, for I tell you it will be a black day for you when you do. But, in the meantime, you perceive that the wind's on the door, and as Fin himself is from home, maybe you'd be civil enough to turn the house, for it's always what Fin does when he's here."

This was a startler even to Cucullin; but he got up, however, and after pulling the middle finger of his right hand until it cracked three times, he went outside, and getting his arms about the house, completely turned it as she had wished. When Fin saw this, he felt a certain description of moisture, which shall be nameless, oozing out through every pore of his skin; but Oonagh, depending upon her woman's wit, felt not a whit daunted.

39

"Arrah, then," said she, "as you are so civil, maybe you'd do another obliging turn for us, as Fin's not here to do it himself. You see, after this long stretch of dry weather we've had, we feel very badly off for want of water. Now, Fin says there's a fine spring-well somewhere under the rocks behind the hill here below, and it was his intention to pull them asunder; but having heard of you, he left the place in such a fury, that he never thought of it. Now, if you try to find it, troth I'd feel it a kindness."

She then brought Cucullin down to see the place, which was then all one solid rock; and, after looking at it for some time, he cracked his right middle finger nine times, and, stooping down, tore a cleft about four hundred feet deep, and a quarter of a mile in length, which has since been christened by the name of Lumford's Glen. This feat nearly threw Oonagh herself off her guard; but what won't a woman's sagacity and presence of mind accomplish?

"You'll now come in," said she, "and eat a bit of such humble fare as we can give you. Fin, even although he and you are enemies, would scorn not to treat you kindly in his own house; and, indeed, if I didn't do it even in his absence, he would not be pleased with me."

She accordingly brought him in, and placing half-a-dozen of the cakes we spoke of before him, together with a can or two of butter, a side of boiled bacon, and a stack of cabbage, she desired him to help himself — for this, be it known, was long before the invention of potatoes. Cucullin, who, by the way, was a glutton as well as a hero, put one of the cakes in his mouth to take a huge whack out of it, when both Fin and Oonagh were stunned with a noise that resembled something between a growl and a yell.

"Blood and fury!" he shouted; "how is this? Here are two of my teeth out! What kind of bread is this you gave me?"

"What's the matter?" said Oonagh coolly.

"Matter!" shouted the other again; "why, here are the two

40

best teeth in my head gone."

"Why," said she, "that's Fin's bread — the only bread he ever eats when at home; but, indeed, I forgot to tell you nobody can eat it but himself, and that child in the cradle there. I thought, however, that, as you were reported to be rather a stout little fellow of your size, you might be able to manage it, and I did not wish to affront a man that thinks himself able to fight Fin. Here's another cake — maybe it's not so hard as that."

Cucullin at the moment was not only hungry, but ravenous, so he accordingly made a fresh set at the second cake, and immediately another yell was heard twice as loud as the first.

"Thunder and giblets!" he roared, "take your bread out of this, or I will not have a tooth in my head; there's another pair of them gone!"

"Well, honest man," replied Oonagh, "if you're not able to eat the bread, say so quietly, and don't be waking the child in the cradle there. There, now, he's awake upon me."

Fin now gave a skirl that startled the giant, as coming from such a youngster as he was represented to be.

"Mother," said he, "I'm hungry — get me something to eat."

Oonagh went over, and putting into his hand a cake *that had no griddle in it,* Fin, whose appetite in the meantime was sharpened by what he saw going forward, soon made it disappear. Cucullin was thunderstruck, and secretly thanked his stars that he had the good fortune to miss meeting Fin, for, as he said to himself, I'd have no chance with a man who could eat such bread as that, which even his son that's in his cradle can munch before my eyes.

"I'd like to take a glimpse at the lad in the cradle," said he to Oonagh; "for I can tell you that the infant who can manage that nutriment is no joke to look at, or to feed of a scarce summer."

"With all the veins of my heart," replied Oonagh; "get up, acushla, and show this decent little man something that won't be unworthy of your father, Fin M'Coul."

Fin, who was dressed for the occasion as much like a boy as possible, got up, and bringing Cucullin out, "Are you strong?" said he.

"Thunder an' ounds!" exclaimed the other, "what a voice in so small a chap!"

"Are you strong?" said Fin again; "are you able to squeeze water out of that white stone?" he asked, putting one into Cucullin's hand. The latter squeezed the stone, but to no purpose; he might pull the rocks of Lumford's Glen asunder, and flatten a thunderbolt, but to squeeze water out of a white stone was beyond his strength. Fin eyed him with great contempt, as he kept straining and squeezing and squeezing and straining, till he got black in the face with the efforts.

"Ah, you're a poor creature!" said Fin. "You a giant! Give me the stone here, and when I'll show what Fin's little son can do, you may then judge of what my daddy himself is."

Fin then took the stone, and slyly exchanging it for the curds, he squeezed the latter until the whey, as clear as water, oozed out in a little shower from his hand.

"I'll now go in," said he "to my cradle; for I scorn to lose my time with anyone that's not able to eat my daddy's bread, or squeeze water out of a stone. Bedad, you had better be off out of this before he comes back; for if he catches you, it's in flummery he'd have you in two minutes."

Cucullin, seeing what he had seen, was of the same opinion himself; his knees knocked together with the terror of Fin's return, and he accordingly hastened in to bid Oonagh farewell, and to assure her, that from that day out, he never wished to hear of, much less to see, her husband.

"I admit fairly that I'm not a match for him," said he, "strong as I am; tell him I will avoid him as I would the plague, and that I will make myself scarce in this part of the country while I live."

Fin, in the meantime, had gone into the cradle, where he lay very quietly, his heart at his mouth with delight that Cucullin was about to take his departure, without discovering the tricks that had been played off on him.

"It's well for you," said Oonagh, "that he doesn't happen to be here, for it's nothing but hawk's meat he'd make of you."

"I know that," says Cucullin; "divil a thing else he'd make of me; but before I go, will you let me feel what kind of teeth they are that can eat griddle-bread like *that*?" – and he pointed to it as he spoke.

"With all pleasure in life," said she; "only, as they're far back in his head, you must put your finger a good way in."

Cucullin was surprised to find such a powerful set of grinders in one so young; but he was still much more so on finding, when he took his hand from Fin's mouth, that he had left the very finger upon which his whole strength depended, behind him. He gave one loud groan, and fell down at once with terror and weakness. This was all Fin wanted, who now knew that his most powerful and bitterest enemy was completely at his mercy. He instantly started out of the cradle, and in a few minutes the great Cucullin, that was for such a length of time the terror of him and all his followers, lay a corpse before him.

Thus did Fin, through the wit and invention of Oonagh, his wife, succeed in overcoming his enemy by stratagem, which he never could have done by force: and thus also it is proved that the women, if they bring us *into* many an unpleasant scrape, can sometimes succeed in getting us *out* of others that are as bad.

7: THE TWELVE WILD GEESE

There was once a king and queen that lived very happily together, and they had twelve sons and not a single daughter. We are always wishing for what we haven't, and don't care for what we have, and so it was with the queen.

One day in winter, when the courtyard was covered with snow, she was looking out of the parlour window, and saw there a calf that was just killed by the butcher, and a raven standing near it.

"Oh," says she, "if I had only a daughter with her skin as white as that snow, her cheeks as red as that blood, and her hair as black as that raven, I'd give away every one of my twelve sons for her." The moment she said the word, she got a great fright, and a shiver went through her, and in an instant after a severe-looking old woman stood before her.

"That was a wicked wish you made," said she, "and to punish you it will be granted. You will have such a daughter as you desire, but the very day of her birth you will lose your other children." She vanished the moment she said the words.

And that very way it turned out. When she expected her delivery, she had her children all in a large room of the palace, with guards all round it, but the very hour her daughter came into the world, the guards inside and outside heard a great whirling and whistling, and the twelve princes were seen flying one after another

45

out through the open window; and away like so many arrows over the woods. Well, the king was in great grief for the loss of his sons, and he would be very enraged with his wife if he only knew that she was so much to blame for it.

Everyone called the little princess Snow-white-and-Rose-red on account of her beautiful complexion. She was the most loving and lovable child that could be seen anywhere.

When she was twelve years old she began to be very sad and lonely, and to torment her mother, asking her about her brothers that she thought were dead, for none up to that time ever told her the exact thing that happened to them. The secret was weighing very heavy on the queen's conscience, and as the little girl persevered in her questions, at last she told her.

"Well, Mother," said she, "it was on my account my poor brothers were changed into wild geese, and are now suffering all sorts of hardship; before the world is a day older, I'll be off to seek them, and try to restore them to their own shapes."

The king and queen had her well watched, but all was no use. Next night she was getting through the woods that surrounded the palace, and she went on and on that night, and till the evening of next day. She had a few cakes with her, and she got nuts, and *mugoreens* (fruit of the sweet briar), and some sweet crabs, as she went along.

At last she came to a nice wooden house just at sunset. There was a fine garden round it, full of the handsomest flowers, and a gate in the hedge. She went in, and saw a table laid out with twelve plates, and twelve knives and forks, and twelve spoons, and there were cakes, and cold wild fowl, and fruit along with the plates, and there was a good fire, and in another long room there were twelve beds. Well, while she was looking about her she heard the gate opening, and footsteps along the walk, and in came twelve young men, and there was great grief on all their faces when they laid eyes on her.

"Oh, what misfortune sent you here?" said the eldest. "For the sake of a girl we were obliged to leave our father's court, and be in the shape of wild geese all day. That's twelve years ago, and we took a solemn oath that we would kill the first young girl that came into our hands. It's a pity to put such an innocent and handsome girl as you are out of the world, but we must keep our oath."

"But," said she, "I'm your only sister, that never knew anything about this till yesterday; and I stole away from our father's and mother's palace last night to find you out and relieve you if I can."

Every one of them clasped his hands and looked down on the floor, and you could hear a pin fall till the eldest cried out, "A curse light on our oath! what shall we do?"

"I'll tell you that," said an old woman that appeared at the instant among them. "Break your wicked oath, which no one should keep. If you attempted to lay an uncivil finger on her I'd change you into twelve *booliaun buis* (stalks of ragweed), but I wish well to you as well as to her. She is appointed to be your deliverer in this way.

She must spin and knit twelve shirts for you out of bog-down, to be gathered by her own hands on the moor just outside of the wood. It will take her five years to do it, and if she once speaks, or laughs, or cries the whole time, you will have to remain wild geese by day till you're called out of the world. So take care of your sister; it is worth your while."

The fairy then vanished, and it was only strife with the brothers to see who would be first to kiss and hug their sister.

So for three long years the poor young princess was occupied pulling bog-down, spinning it, and knitting it into shirts, and at the end of the three years she had eight made. During all that time, she never spoke a word, nor laughed, nor cried: the last was the hardest to refrain from.

One fine day she was sitting in the garden spinning, when in sprung a fine greyhound and bounded up to her, and laid his paws on her shoulder, and licked her forehead and her hair. The next minute a beautiful young prince rode up to the little garden gate, took off his hat, and asked for leave to come in. She gave him a little nod, and in he walked.

He made ever so many apologies for intruding, and asked her ever so many questions, but not a word could he get out of her. He loved her so much from the first moment that he could not leave her till he told her he was king of a country just bordering on the forest, and he begged her to come home with him, and be his wife.

She couldn't help loving him as much as he did her, and though she shook her head very often, and was very sorry to leave her brothers, at last she nodded her head, and put her hand in his. She knew well enough that the good fairy and her brothers would be able to find her out. Before she went she brought out a basket holding all her bog-down, and another holding the eight shirts. The attendants took charge of these, and the prince placed her before him on his horse.

The only thing that disturbed him while riding along was the displeasure his stepmother would feel at what he had done. However, he was full master at home, and as soon as he arrived he sent for the bishop, got his bride nicely dressed and the marriage was celebrated, the bride answering by signs. He knew by her manners she was of high birth, and no two could be fonder of each other.

The wicked stepmother did all she could to make mischief, saying she was sure she was only a woodman's daughter; but nothing could disturb the young king's opinion of his wife.

In good time the young queen was delivered of a beautiful boy, and the king was so glad he hardly knew what to do for joy. All the grandeur of the christening and the happiness of the parents tormented the bad woman more than I can tell you, and she determined to put a stop to all their comfort.

She got a sleeping posset given to the young mother, and while

FAIRY TALES OF IRELAND

she was thinking and thinking how she could best make away with
the child, she saw a wicked-looking wolf in the garden, looking
up at her, and licking his chops. She lost no time, but snatched the
child from the arms of the sleeping woman, and pitched it out. The
beast caught it in his mouth, and was over the garden fence in a
minute. The wicked woman then pricked her own fingers, and
dabbed the blood round the mouth of the sleeping mother.

Well, the young king was just then coming into the big courtyard from hunting, and as soon as he entered the house, she
beckoned to him, shed a few crocodile tears, began to cry and
wring her hands, and hurried him along the passage to the bed-
chamber.

Oh, wasn't the poor king frightened when he saw the queen's
mouth bloody, and missed his child? It would take two hours to tell
you the devilment of the old queen, the confusion and fright, and
grief of the young king and queen, the bad opinion he began to
feel of his wife, and the struggle she had to keep down her bitter
sorrow, and not give way to it by speaking or lamenting.

The young king would not allow anyone to be called, and
ordered his stepmother to give out that the child fell from the
mother's arms at the window, and that a wild beast ran off with it.
The wicked woman pretended to do so, but she told underhand to
everybody she spoke to what the king and herself saw in the bed-
chamber.

The young queen was the most unhappy woman in the three
kingdoms for a long time, between sorrow for her child and her
husband's bad opinion; still she neither spoke nor cried, and she
gathered bog-down and went on with the shirts.

Often the twelve wild geese would be seen lighting on the trees
in the park or on the smooth sod, and looking in at her windows.
So she worked on to get the shirts finished, but another year was at
an end, and she had the twelfth shirt finished except one arm,
when she was obliged to take to her bed, and a beautiful girl was

50

born.

Now the king was on his guard, and he would not let the mother and child be left alone for a minute; but the wicked woman bribed some of the attendants, set others asleep, gave the sleepy posset to the queen, and had a person watching to snatch the child away, and kill it.

But what should she see but the same wolf in the garden looking up, and licking his chops again? Out went the child, and away with it flew the wolf, and she smeared the sleeping mother's mouth and face with blood, and then roared, and bawled, and cried out to the king and to everybody she met, and the room was filled, and everyone was sure the young queen had just devoured her own babe.

The poor mother thought now her life would leave her. She was in such a state she could neither think nor pray, but she sat like a stone, and worked away at the arm of the twelfth shirt.

The king was for taking her to the house in the wood where he found her but the stepmother, and the lords of the court, and the judges would not hear of it, and she was condemned to be burned in the big courtyard at three o'clock the same day. When the hour drew near, the king went to the farthest part of his palace, and there was no more unhappy man in his kingdom at that hour.

When the executioners came and led her off, she took the pile of shirts in her arms. There was still a few stitches wanted, and while they were tying her to the stake she still worked on. At the last stitch she seemed overcome and dropped a tear on her work, but the moment after she sprang up, and shouted out, "I am innocent; call my husband!"

The executioners stayed their hands, except one wicked-disposed creature, who set fire to the faggot next him, and while all were struck in amaze, there was a rushing of wings, and in a moment the twelve wild geese were standing around the pile. Before you could count twelve, she flung a shirt over each bird, and there in the twinkling of an eye were twelve of the finest young men that could be collected out of a thousand. While some were untying their sister, the eldest, taking a strong stake in his hand, struck the busy executioner such a blow that he never needed another.

While they were comforting the young queen, and the king was hurrying to the spot, a fine-looking woman appeared among them holding the babe on one arm and the little prince by the hand.

There was nothing but crying for joy, and laughing for joy, and hugging and kissing, and when any one had time to thank the good fairy, who in the shape of a wolf, carried the child away, she was not to be found. Never was such happiness enjoyed in any palace that ever was built, and if the wicked queen and her helpers were not torn by wild horses, they richly deserved it.

8: THE LAZY BEAUTY AND HER AUNTS

There was once a poor widow woman, who had a daughter that was as handsome as the day, and as lazy as a pig, saving your presence. The poor mother was the most industrious person in the townland, and was a particularly good hand at the spinning-wheel. It was the wish of her heart that her daughter should be as handy as herself; but she'd get up late, eat her breakfast before she'd finished her prayers, and then go about dawdling, and anything she handled seemed to be burning her fingers. She drawled her words as if it was a great trouble to her to speak, or as if her tongue was as lazy as her body. Many a heart-scald her poor mother got with her, and still she was only improving like dead fowl in August.

Well, one morning that things were as bad as they could be, and the poor woman was giving tongue at the rate of a mill-clapper, who should be riding by but the king's son.

"Oh dear, oh dear, good woman!" said he, "you must have a very bad child to make you scold so terribly. Sure it can't be this handsome girl that vexed you!"

"Oh, please your Majesty, not at all," says the old dissembler. "I was only checking her for working herself too much. Would your Majesty believe it? She spins three pounds of flax in a day, weaves it into linen the next, and makes it all into shirts the day after."

"My gracious," says the prince, "she's the very lady that will just fill my mother's eye, and herself's the greatest spinner in the kingdom. Will you put on your daughter's bonnet and cloak, if you please, ma'am, and set her behind me? Why, my mother will be so delighted with her, that perhaps she'll make her her daughter-in-law in a week, that is, if the young woman herself is agreeable."

Well, between the confusion, and the joy, and the fear of being found out, the women didn't know what to do; and before they could make up their minds, young Anty (Anastasia) was set behind the prince, and away he and his attendants went, and a good heavy purse was left behind with the mother. She *pullillued* a long time after all was gone, in dread of something bad happening to the poor girl.

The prince couldn't judge of the girl's breeding or wit from the few answers he pulled out of her. The queen was struck in a heap when she saw a young country girl sitting behind her son, but when she saw her handsome face, and heard all she could do, she didn't think she could make too much of her. The prince took an opportunity of whispering to her that if she didn't object to be his wife she must strive to please his mother.

Well, the evening went by, and the prince and Anty were getting fonder and fonder of one another, but the thought of the spinning used to send the cold to her heart every moment. When bedtime came, the old queen went along with her to a beautiful bedroom, and when she was bidding her good night, she pointed to a heap of fine flax, and said:

"You may begin as soon as you like tomorrow morning, and I'll expect to see these three pounds in nice thread the morning after."

Little did the poor girl sleep that night. She kept crying and lamenting that she didn't mind her mother's advice better. When she was left alone next morning, she began with a heavy heart;

and though she had a nice mahogany wheel and the finest flax you
ever saw, the thread was breaking every moment. One while it
was as fine as a cobweb, and the next as coarse as a little boy's
whipcord. At last she pushed her chair back, let her hands fall in
her lap, and burst out a-crying.

A small, old woman with surprising big feet appeared before
her at the same moment, and said, "What ails you, you handsome
colleen?"

"An' haven't I all that flax to spin before tomorrow morning, and I'll never be able to have even five yards of fine thread of it put together."

"An' would you think bad to ask poor *Colliagh Cushmōr* (Old woman Big-foot) to your wedding with the young prince? If you promise me that, all your three pounds will be made into the finest of thread while you're taking your sleep tonight."

"Indeed, you must be there and welcome, and I'll honour you all the days of your life."

"Very well; stay in your room till tea-time, and tell the queen she may come in for her thread as early as she likes tomorrow morning."

It was all as she said; and the thread was finer and evener than the gut you see with fly-fishers.

"My brave girl you were!" says the queen. "I'll get my own mahogany loom brought into you, but you needn't do anything more today. Work and rest, work and rest, is my motto. Tomorrow you'll weave all this thread, and who knows what may happen?"

The poor girl was more frightened this time than the last, and she was so afraid to lose the prince. She didn't even know how to put the warp in the gears, nor how to use the shuttle, and she was sitting in the greatest grief, when a little woman, who was mighty well-shouldered about the hips, all at once appeared to her, told her her name was *Colliach Cromanmōr,* and made the same bargain with her as Colliach Cushmōr.

Great was the queen's pleasure when she found early in the morning a web as fine and white as the finest paper you ever saw.

56

"The darling you were!" says she. "Take your ease with the ladies and gentlemen today, and if you have all this made into nice shirts tomorrow you may present one of them to my son, and be married to him out of hand."

Oh, wouldn't you pity poor Anty the next day, she was now so near the prince, and, maybe, would be soon so far from him. But she waited as patiently as she could with scissors, needle, and thread in hand, till a minute after noon. Then she was rejoiced to see the third woman appear. She had a big red nose, and informed Anty that people called her *Shron Mor Rua* on that account. She was up to her as good as the others, for a dozen fine shirts were lying on the table when the queen paid her an early visit.

Now there was nothing talked of but the wedding, and I needn't tell you it was grand. The poor mother was there along with the rest, and at the dinner the old queen could talk of nothing but the lovely shirts, and how happy herself and the bride would be after the honeymoon, spinning, and weaving, and sewing shirts and shirts without end. The bridegroom didn't like the discourse, and the bride liked it less, and he was going to say something, when the footman came up to the head of the table and said to the bride:

"Your ladyship's aunt, Colliach Cuchmōr, bade me ask might she come in." The bride blushed and wished she was seven miles under the floor, but well became the prince.

"Tell Mrs. Cushmōr," said he, "that any relation of my bride's will be always heartily welcome wherever she and I are."

In came the woman with the big foot, and got a seat near the prince. The old queen didn't like it much, and after a few words she asked rather spitefully:

"Dear ma'am, what's the reason your foot is so big?"

"*Musha,* faith, your majesty, I was standing almost all my life at the spinning-wheel, and that's the reason."

"I declare to you, my darling," said the prince, "I'll never allow you to spend one hour at the same spinning-wheel."

The same footman said again, "Your ladyship's aunt, Colliach Cromanmōr, wishes to come in, if the genteels and yourself have no objection." Very *sharoose* (displeased) was Princess Anty, but the prince sent her welcome, and she took her seat, and drank healths apiece to the company.

"May I ask, ma'am?" says the old queen, "why you're so wide half-way between the head and the feet?"

"That, your majesty, is owing to sitting all my life at the loom."

"By my sceptre," says the prince, "my wife shall never sit there an hour."

The footman again came up. "Your ladyship's aunt, Colliach Shron Mor Rua, is asking leave to come into the banquet." More blushing on the bride's face, but the bridegroom spoke out cordially.

"Tell Mrs. Shron Mor Rua she's doing us an honour."

In came the old woman, and great respect she got near the top of the table, but the people down low put up their tumblers and glasses to their noses to hide the grins.

"Ma'am," says the old queen, "will you tell us, if you please, why your nose is so big and red?"

"Throth, your majesty, my head was bent down over the stitching all my life, and all the blood in my body ran into my nose."

"My darling," said the prince to Anty, "if ever I see a needle in your hand, I'll run a hundred miles from you."

"And in troth, girls and boys, though it's a diverting story, I don't think the moral is good; and if any of you *thuckeens* go about imitating Anty in her laziness, you'll find it won't thrive with you as it did with her. She was beautiful beyond compare, which none of you are, and she had three powerful fairies to help her besides. There's no fairies now, and no prince or lord to ride by, and catch you idling or working; and maybe, after all, the prince and herself were not so very happy when the cares of the world or old age came on them."

Thus was the tale ended by poor old *Shebale* (Sybilla), Father Murphy's housekeeper, in Coolbawn, Barony of Bantry, about half a century since.

9: THE HAUGHTY PRINCESS

There was once a very worthy king, whose daughter was the greatest beauty that could be seen far or near, but she was as proud as Lucifer, and no king or prince would she agree to marry. Her father was tired out at last, and invited every king and prince, and duke, and earl that he knew or didn't know to come to his court to give her one trial more. They all came, and next day after breakfast they stood in a row on the lawn, and the princess walked along in the front of them to make her choice.

One was fat, and says she, "I won't have you, Beer-barrel!" One was tall and thin, and to him she said, "I won't have you, Ramrod!" To a white-faced man she said, "I won't have you, Pale Death;" and to a red-cheeked man she said, "I won't have you, Cockscomb!"

She stopped a little before the last of all for he was a fine man in face and form. She wanted to find some defect in him, but he had nothing remarkable but a ring of brown curling hair under his chin. She admired him a little, and then carried it off with, "I won't have you, Whiskers!"

So all went away, and the king was so vexed, he said to her, "Now to punish your *impidence,* I'll give you to the first beggar-man or singing *sthronshuch* that calls;" and, as sure as the hearth-money, a fellow all over rags, and hair that came to his shoulders,

and a bushy red beard all over his face, came next morning, and began to sing before the parlour window.

When the song was over, the hall door was opened, the singer asked in, the priest brought, and the princess married to Beardy. She roared and she bawled, but her father didn't mind her.

"There," says he to the bridegroom, "is five guineas for you. Take your wife out of my sight, and never let me lay eyes on you or her again."

Off he led her, and dismal enough she was. The only thing that gave her relief was the tone of her husband's voice and his genteel manners.

"Whose wood is this?" said she, as they were going through one.

"It belongs to the king you called Whiskers yesterday." He gave her the same answer about meadows and cornfields and at last a fine city.

"Ah, what a fool I was!" said she to herself. "He was a fine man, and I might have him for a husband."

At last they were coming up to a poor cabin. "Why are you bringing me here?" says the poor lady.

"This was my house," said he, "and now it's your's." She began to cry, but she was tired and hungry, and she went in with him.

Ovoch! there was neither a table laid out, nor a fire burning, and she was obliged to help her husband to light it, and boil their dinner, and clean up the place after; and next day he made her put on a stuff gown and a cotton handkerchief.

When she had her house readied up, and no business to keep her employed, he brought home *sallies* (willows), peeled them, and showed her how to make baskets. But the hard twigs bruised her delicate fingers, and she began to cry. Well, then he asked her to mend their clothes, but the needle drew blood from her fingers, and she cried again. He couldn't bear to see her tears, so he bought a creel of earthenware, and sent her to the market to sell them.

This was the hardest trial of all, but she looked so handsome and sorrowful, and had such a nice air about her, that all her pans, and jugs, and plates, and dishes were gone before noon, and the only mark of her old pride she showed was a slap she gave a buckeen, across the face when he *axed* her to go in an' take share of a quart.

Well, her husband was so glad, he sent her with another creel the next day; but faith! her luck was after deserting her. A drunken huntsman came up riding, and his beast got in among her ware, and made *brishe* of every mother's son of 'em. She went home cryin', and her husband wasn't at all pleased.

"I see," said he, "you're not fit for business. Come along, I'll get you a kitchen-maid's place in the palace. I know the cook."

So the poor thing was obliged to stifle her pride once more. She was kept busy, and the footman and the butler would be very

impudent about looking for a kiss, but she let a screech out of her the first attempt was made, and the cook gave the fellow such a lambasting with the besom that he made no second offer. She went home to her husband every night, and she carried broken victuals wrapped in papers in her side pockets.

A week after she got service there was great bustle in the kitchen. The king was going to be married, but no one knew who the bride was to be. Well, in the evening the cook filled the princess's pockets with cold meat and puddings, and, says she, "Before you go, let us have a look at the great doings in the big parlour." So they came near the door to get a peep, and who should come out but the king himself, as handsome as you please, and no other but King Whiskers himself.

"Your handsome helper must pay for her peeping," said he to the cook, "and dance a jig with me."

Whether she would or no, he held her hand and brought her into the parlour. The fiddlers struck up, and away went *him* with *her*. But they hadn't danced two steps when the meat and the *puddens* flew out of her pockets. Everyone roared out, and she flew to the door, crying piteously. But she was soon caught by the king, and taken into the back parlour.

"Don't you know me, my darling?" said he. "I'm both King Whiskers, your husband the ballad-singer, and the drunken huntsman. Your father knew me well enough when he gave you to me, and all was to drive your pride out of you."

Well, she didn't know how she was with fright, and shame, and joy. Love was uppermost anyhow, for she laid her head on her husband's breast and cried like a child.

The maids-of-honour soon had her away and dressed her as fine as hands and pins could do it; and there were her mother and father, too; and while the company were wondering what end of the handsome girl and the king, he and his queen, who they didn't know in her fine clothes, and the other king and queen, came in, and such rejoicings and fine doings as there was, none of us will ever see, anyway.

10: FAR DARRIG IN DONEGAL

Pat Diver, the tinker, was a man well-accustomed to a wandering life, and to strange shelters; he had shared the beggar's blanket in smoky cabins; he had crouched beside the still in many a nook and corner where poteen was made on the wild Innishowen mountains; he had even slept on the bare heather, or on the ditch, with no roof over him but the vault of heaven; yet were all his nights of adventure tame and commonplace when compared with one especial night.

During the day preceding that night, he had mended all the kettles and saucepans in Moville and Greencastle, and was on his way to Culdaff, when night overtook him on a lonely mountain road.

He knocked at one door after another asking for a night's lodging, while he jingled the halfpence in his pocket, but was everywhere refused.

Where was the boasted hospitality of Innishowen, which he had never before known to fail? It was of no use to be able to pay when the people seemed so churlish. Thus thinking, he made his way towards a light a little farther on, and knocked at another cabin door.

An old man and woman were seated one at each side of the fire.

"Will you be pleased to give me a night's lodging, sir?" asked

66

Pat respectfully.

"Can you tell a story?" returned the old man.

"No, then, sir, I canna say I'm good at story-telling," replied the puzzled tinker.

"Then you maun just gang farther, for none but them that can tell a story will get in here."

This reply was made in so decided a tone that Pat did not attempt to repeat his appeal, but turned away reluctantly to resume his weary journey.

"A story, indeed," muttered he. "Auld wives fables to please the weans!"

As he took his bundle of tinkering implements, he observed a barn standing rather behind the dwelling-house, and, aided by the rising moon, he made his way towards it.

It was a clean, roomy barn, with a piled-up heap of straw in one corner. Here was a shelter not to be despised; so Pat crept under the straw and was soon asleep.

He could not have slept very long when he was awakened by the tramp of feet, and, peeping cautiously through a crevice in his straw covering, he saw four immensely tall men enter the barn, dragging a body which they threw roughly upon the floor.

They next lighted a fire in the middle of the barn, and fastened the corpse by the feet with a great rope to a beam in the roof. One of them began to turn it slowly before the fire.

"Come on," said he, addressing a gigantic fellow, the tallest of the four – "I'm tired; you be to tak' your turn."

"Faix an' troth, I'll no' turn him," replied the big man.

"There's Pat Diver in under the straw, why wouldn't he tak' his turn?"

With hideous clamour the four men called the wretched Pat, who, seeing there was no escape, thought it was his wisest plan to come forth as he was bidden.

"Now, Pat," said they, "you'll turn the corpse, but if you let

—

him burn you'll be tied up there and roasted in his place."

Pat's hair stood on end, and the cold perspiration poured from his forehead, but there was nothing for it but to perform his dreadful task.

Seeing him fairly embarked in it, the tall men went away.

Soon, however, the flames rose so high as to singe the rope, and the corpse fell with a great thud upon the fire, scattering the ashes and embers, and extracting a howl of anguish from the miserable cook, who rushed to the door, and ran for his life.

He ran on until he was ready to drop with fatigue, when, seeing a drain overgrown with tall, rank grass, he thought he would creep in there and lie hidden till morning.

But he was not many minutes in the drain before he heard the heavy tramping again, and the four men came up with their burthen, which they laid down on the edge of the drain.

"I'm tired," said one, to the giant; "it's your turn to carry him a piece now."

"Faix and troth, I'll no' carry him," replied he, "but there's Pat Diver in the drain, why wouldn't he come out and tak' his turn?"

"Come out, Pat, come out," roared all the men, and Pat, almost dead with fright, crept out.

He staggered on under weight of the corpse until he reached Kiltown Abbey, a ruin festooned with ivy, where the brown owl hooted all night long, and the forgotten dead slept around the walls under dense, matted tangles of brambles and ben-weed.

No one ever buried there now, but Pat's tall companions turned into the wild graveyard, and began digging a grave.

Pat, seeing them thus engaged, thought he might once more try to escape, and climbed up into a hawthorn tree in the fence, hoping to be hidden in the boughs.

"I'm tired," said the man who was digging the grave; "here, take the spade," addressing the big man, "it's your turn."

"Faix an' troth, it's no' my turn," replied he, as before. "There's Pat Diver in the tree, why wouldn't he come down and tak' his turn?"

Pat came down to take the spade, but just then the cocks in the little farmyards and cabins round the abbey began to crow, and the men looked at one another.

"We must go," said they, "and well is it for you, Pat Diver, that the cocks crowed, for if they had not, you'd just ha' been bundled into that grave with the corpse."

Two months passed, and Pat had wandered far and wide over the county Donegal, when he chanced to arrive at Raphoe during a fair.

Among the crowd that filled the Diamond he came suddenly on the big man.

"How are you, Pat Diver?" said he, bending down to look into the tinker's face.

"You've the advantage of me, sir, for I havna' the pleasure of knowing you," faltered Pat.

"Do you not know me, Pat?" Whisper — "When you go back to Innishowen, you'll have a story to tell!"

11: DONALD AND HIS NEIGHBOURS

Hudden and Dudden and Donald O'Nery were near neighbours in the barony of Balinconlig, and ploughed with three bullocks; but the two former, envying the present prosperity of the latter, determined to kill his bullock, to prevent his farm being properly cultivated and laboured, that going back in the world he might be induced to sell his lands, which they meant to get possession of. Poor Donald finding his bullock killed, immediately skinned it, and throwing the skin over his shoulder, with the fleshy side out, set off to the next town with it, to dispose of it to the best of his advantage.

Going along the road a magpie flew on the top of the hide, and began picking it, chattering all the time. The bird had been taught to speak, and imitate the human voice, and Donald, thinking he understood some words it was saying, put round his hand and caught hold of it. Having got possession of it, he put it under his greatcoat, and so went to town.

Having sold the hide, he went into an inn to take a dram, and following the landlady into the cellar, he gave the bird a squeeze which made it chatter some broken accents that surprised her very much.

"What is that I hear?" said she to Donald. "I think it is talk, and yet I do not understand."

71

"Indeed," said Donald, "it is a bird I have that tells me everything, and I always carry it with me to know when there is any danger. Faith," says he, "it says you have far better liquor than you are giving me."

"That is strange," said she, going to another cask of better quality, and asking him if he would sell the bird.

"I will," said Donald, "if I get enough for it."

"I will fill your hat with silver if you leave it with me."

Donald was glad to hear the news, and taking the silver, set off, rejoicing at his good luck. He had not been long at home until he met with Hudden and Dudden.

"Mr," said he, "you thought you had done me a bad turn, but you could not have done me a better; for look here, what I have got for the hide," showing them a hatful of silver; "you never saw such a demand for hides in your life as there is at present."

Hudden and Dudden that very night killed their bullocks, and set out the next morning to sell their hides. On coming to the place they went through all the merchants, but could only get a trifle for them; at last they had to take what they could get, and came home in a great rage, and vowing revenge on poor Donald.

He had a pretty good guess how matters would turn out, and he being under the kitchen window, he was afraid they would rob him, or perhaps kill him when asleep, and on that account when he was going to bed he left his old mother in his place, and lay down in her bed, which was in the other side of the house, and they taking the old woman for Donald, choked her in her bed, but he making some noise, they had to retreat, and leave the money behind them, which grieved them very much.

However, by daybreak, Donald got his mother on his back, and carried her to town. Stopping at a well, he fixed his mother with her staff, as if she was stooping for a drink, and then went into a public house convenient and called for a dram.

"I wish," said he to a woman that stood near him, "you

would tell my mother to come in; she is at yon well trying to get a drink, and she is hard of hearing; if she does not observe you, give her a little shake and tell her that I want her."

The woman called her several times, but she seemed to take no notice; at length she went to her and shook her by the arm, but when she let her go again, she tumbled on her head into the well, and, as the woman thought, was drowned. She, in her great surprise and fear at the accident, told Donald what had happened.

"O mercy," said he, "what is this?" He ran and pulled her out of the well, weeping and lamenting all the time, and acting in such a manner that you would imagine that he had lost his senses.

The woman, on the other hand, was far worse than Donald, for his grief was only feigned, but she imagined herself to be the cause of the old woman's death.

The inhabitants of the town, hearing what had happened, agreed to make Donald up a good sum of money for his loss, as the accident happened in their place, and Donald brought a greater sum home

with him than he got for the magpie. They buried Donald's mother, and as soon as he saw Hudden and Dudden he showed them the last purse of money he had got.

"You thought to kill me last night," said he, "but it was good for me it happened on my mother, for I got all the purse for her to make gunpowder."

That very night Hudden and Dudden killed their mothers, and the next morning set off with them to town. On coming to the town with their burthen on their backs, they went up and down crying, "Who will buy old wives for gunpowder," so that everyone laughed at them, and the boys at last clotted them out of the place. They then saw the cheat, and vowed revenge on Donald, buried the old women, and set off in pursuit of him.

Coming to his house they found him sitting at his breakfast, and seizing him, put him in a sack, and went to drown him in a river at some distance. As they were going along the highway they raised a hare, which they saw had but three feet, and throwing off the sack, ran after her, thinking by her appearance she would be easily taken.

In their absence there came a drover that way, and hearing Donald singing in the sack, wondered greatly what could be the matter.

"What is the reason," said he, "that you are singing, and you confined?"

"O, I am going to heaven," said Donald, "and in a short time I expect to be free from trouble."

"O dear," said the drover, "what will I give you if you let me to your place?"

"Indeed, I do not know," said he, "it would take a good sum."

"I have not much money," said the drover, "but I have twenty head of fine cattle, which I will give you to exchange places with me."

"Well," says Donald, "I do not care if I should lose the sack, and I will come out."

In a moment the drover liberated him, and went into the sack himself, and Donald drove home the fine heifers, and left them in his pasture.

Hudden and Dudden having caught the hare, returned, and getting the sack on one of their backs, carried Donald, as they thought, to the river and threw him in, where he immediately sank. They then marched home, intending to take immediate possession of Donald's property, but how great was their surprise when they found him safe at home before them, with such a fine head of cattle, whereas they knew he had none before.

"Donald," said they, "what is all this? We thought you were drowned, and yet you are here before us."

"Ah!" said he, "if I had but help along with me when you threw me in, it would have been the best job ever I met with, for all the sight of cattle and gold that ever was seen is there, and no one to own them, but I was not able to manage more than what you see, and I could show you the spot where you might get hundreds."

"They both swore they would be his friends, and Donald accordingly led them to a very deep part of the river, and lifted up a stone.

"Now," said he, "watch this," throwing it into the stream; "there is the very place, and go in, one of you first, and if you want help, you have nothing to do but call."

Hudden jumping in, and sinking to the bottom, rose up again, and making a bubbling noise, as those do that are drowning, attempted to speak, but could not.

"What is that he is saying now?" says Dudden.

"Faith," says Donald, "he is calling for help; don't you hear him? Stand about," said he, running back, "till I leap in. I know how to do it better than any of you."

Dudden, to have the advantage of him, jumped in off the bank,

and was drowned along with Hudden, and this was the end of
Hudden and Dudden.

12: MASTER AND MAN

Billy Mac Daniel was once as likely a young man as ever shook his brogue at a patron,* emptied a quart, or handled a shillelagh; fearing for nothing but the want of drink; caring for nothing but who should pay for it; and thinking of nothing but how to make fun over it; drunk or sober, a word and a blow was ever the way with Billy Mac Daniel; and a mighty easy way it is of either getting into or of ending a dispute. More is the pity that, through the means of his thinking, and fearing, and caring for nothing, this same Billy Mac Daniel fell into bad company; for surely the good people are the worst of all company anyone could come across.

It so happened that Billy was going home one clear frosty night not long after Christmas; the moon was round and bright; but although it was as fine a night as heart could wish for, he felt pinched with cold.

"By my word," chattered Billy, "a drop of good liquor would be no bad thing to keep a man's soul from freezing in him; and I wish I had a full measure of the best."

"Never wish it twice, Billy," said a little man in a three-cornered hat, bound all about with gold lace, and with great silver buckles in his shoes, so big that it was a wonder how he could carry them, and he held out a glass as big as himself, filled with as good

*A Festival held in honour of some patron saint.

78

liquor as ever eye looked on or lip tasted.

"Success, my little fellow," said Billy Mac Daniel, nothing daunted, though well he knew the little man to belong to the *good people*; "here's your health, anyway, and thank you kindly; no matter who pays for the drink;" and he took the glass and drained it to the very bottom without ever taking a second breath to it.

"Success," said the little man; "and you're heartily welcome, Billy; but don't think to cheat me as you have done others – out with your purse and pay me like a gentleman."

"Is it I pay you?" said Billy; "could I not just take you up and put you in my pocket as easily as a blackberry?"

"Billy Mac Daniel," said the little man, getting very angry, "you shall be my servant for seven years and a day, and that is the way I will be paid; so make ready to follow me."

When Billy heard this he began to be very sorry for having used such bold words towards the little man; and he felt himself, yet could not tell how, obliged to follow the little man the live-long night about the country, up and down, and over hedge and ditch, and through bog and brake, without any rest.

When morning began to dawn the little man turned round to him and said, "You may now go home, Billy, but on your peril don't fail to meet me in the Fort-field tonight; or if you do it may be the worse for you in the long run. If I find you a good servant, you will find me an indulgent master."

Home went Billy Mac Daniel; and though he was tired and weary enough, never a wink of sleep could he get for thinking of the little man; but he was afraid not to do his bidding, so up he got in the evening, and away he went to the Fort-field. He was not long there before the little man came towards him and said, "Billy, I want to go a long journey tonight; so saddle one of my horses, and you may saddle another for yourself, as you are to go along with me, and may be tired after your walk last night."

Billy thought this very considerate of his master, and thanked him accordingly: "But," said he, "if I may be so bold, sir, I would ask which is the way to your stable, for never a thing do I see but the fort here, and the old thorn tree in the corner of the field, and the stream running at the bottom of the hill, with the bit of bog over against us."

"Ask no questions, Billy" said the little man," "but go over to that bit of a bog, and bring me two of the strongest. rushes you can find.

Billy did accordingly, wondering what the little man would be at; and he picked two of the stoutest rushes he could find, with a little bunch of brown blossom stuck at the side of each, and brought them back to his master.

"Get up, Billy," said the little man, taking one of the rushes from him and striding across it.

"Where shall I get up, please your honour?" said Billy.

"Why, upon horseback, like me, to be sure," said the little man.

"Is it after making a fool of me you'd be," said Billy, "bidding me get a horseback upon that bit of rush? Maybe you want to persuade me that the rush I pulled but a while ago out of the bog over there is a horse?"

"Up! up! and no words," said the little man, looking very angry; "the best horse you ever rode was but a fool to it." So Billy, thinking all this was in joke, and fearing to vex his master, straddled across the rush.

"Borram! Borram! Borram!" cried the little man three times (which, in English, means to become great), and Billy did the same after him; presently the rushes swelled up into fine horses, and away they went full speed; but Billy, who had put the rush between his legs, without much minding how he did it, found himself sitting on horseback the wrong way, which was rather awkward, with his face to the horse's tail; and so quickly had his

steed started off with him that he had no power to turn round, and there was therefore nothing for it but to hold on by the tail.

At last they came to their journey's end, and stopped at the gate of a fine house. "Now, Billy," said the little man, "do as you see me do, and follow me close; but as you did not know your horse's head from his tail, mind that your own head does not spin round until you can't tell whether you are standing on it or on your heels: for remember that old liquor, though able to make a cat speak, can make a man dumb."

The little man then said some queer kind of words, out of which Billy could make no meaning; but he contrived to say them after him for all that; and in they both went through the keyhole of the door, and through one keyhole after another, until they got into the wine cellar, which was well stored with all kinds of wine.

The little man fell to drinking as hard as he could, and Billy, noway disliking the example, did the same. "The best of masters are you surely," said Billy to him; "no matter who is the next; and well pleased will I be with your service if you continue to give me plenty to drink."

81

"I have made no bargain with you," said the little man, "and will make none; but up and follow me." Away they went, through keyhole after keyhole; and each mounting upon the rush which he left at the hall door, scampered off, kicking the clouds before them like snowballs, as soon as the words, "Borram, Borram, Borram", had passed their lips.

When they came back to the Fort-field the little man dismissed Billy, bidding him to be there the next night at the same hour. Thus did they go on, night after night, shaping their course one night here, and another night there; sometimes north, and sometimes east, and sometimes south, until there was not a gentleman's wine cellar in all Ireland they had not visited, and could tell the flavour of every wine in it as well, ay, better than the butler himself.

One night when Billy Mac Daniel met the little man as usual in the Fort-field, and was going to the bog to fetch the horses for their journey, his master said to him, "Billy, I shall want another horse tonight, for maybe we may bring back more company than we take." So Billy, who now knew better than to question any order given to him by his master, brought a third rush, much wondering who it might be that would travel back in their company, and whether he was about to have a fellow-servant. "If I have," thought Billy, "he shall go and fetch the horses from the bog every night; for I don't see why I am not, every inch of me, as good a gentleman as my master."

Well, away they went, Billy leading the third horse, and never stopped until they came to a snug farmer's house, in the county Limerick, close under the old castle of Carrigogunniel, that was built, they say, by the great Brian Boru. Within the house there was great carousing going forward, and the little man stopped outside for some time to listen; then turning round all of a sudden, said, "Billy, I will be a thousand years old tomorrow!"

"God bless us, sir," said Billy; "will you?"

"Don't say these words again, Billy," said the little old man, "or you will be my ruin for ever. Now Billy, as I will be a thousand years in the world tomorrow, I think it is full time for mc to gct married."

"I think so too, without any kind of doubt at all," said Billy, "if ever you mean to marry."

"And to that purpose," said the little man, "have I come all the way to Carrigogunniel; for in this house, this very night, is young Darby Riley going to be married to Bridget Rooney; and as she is a tall and comely girl, and has come of decent people, I think of marrying her myself, and taking her off with me."

"And what will Darby Riley say to that?" said Billy.

"Silence!" said the little man, putting on a mighty severe look; "I did not bring you here with me to ask questions;" and without holding further argument, he began saying the queer words which had the power of passing him through the keyhole as free as air, and which Billy thought himself mighty clever to be able to say after him.

In they both went; and for the better viewing the company, the little man perched himself up as nimbly as a cocksparrow upon one of the big beams which went across the house over all their heads, and Billy did the same upon another facing him; but not being much accustomed to roosting in such a place, his legs hung down as untidy as maybe, and it was quite clear he had not taken pattern after the way in which the little man had bundled himself up together. If the little man had been a tailor all his life he could not have sat more contentedly upon his haunches.

There they were, both master and man, looking down upon the fun that was going forward; and under them were the priest and piper, and the father of Darby Riley, with Darby's two brothers and his uncle's son; and there were both the father and the mother of Bridget Rooney, and proud enough the old people were that night of their daughter, as good right they had; and her four sisters, with bran' new ribbons in their caps, and her three brothers all looking as clean and as clever as any three boys in Munster, and there were uncles and aunts, and gossips and cousins enough besides to make a full house of it; and plenty was there to eat and drink on the table for everyone of them, if they had been double the number.

Now it happened, just as Mrs Rooney had helped his reverence to the first cut of the pig's head which was placed before her, beautifully bolstered up with white savoys, that the bride gave a sneeze, which made everyone at table start, but not a soul said "God bless us". All thinking that the priest would have done so, as he ought if he had done his duty, no one wished to take the word out of his mouth, which, unfortunately, was preoccupied with pig's head and greens. And after a moment's pause the fun and merriment of the bridal feast went on without the pious benediction.

Of this circumstance both Billy and his master were no inattentive spectators from their exalted stations. "Ha!" exclaimed the little man, throwing one leg from under him with a joyous flourish, and his eye twinkled with a strange light, whilst his eyebrows became elevated into the curvature of Gothic arches; "Ha!" said he, leering down at the bride, and then up at Billy, "I have half of her now, surely. Let her sneeze but twice more, and she is mine, in spite of priest, mass-book, and Darby Riley."

Again the fair Bridget sneezed; but it was so gently, and she blushed so much, that few except the little man took, or seemed to take, any notice; and no one thought of saying "God bless us".

Billy all this time regarded the poor girl with a most rueful expression of countenance; for he could not help thinking what a terrible thing it was for a nice young girl of nineteen, with large blue eyes, transparent skin, and dimpled cheeks, suffused with health and joy, to be obliged to marry an ugly little bit of a man, who was a thousand years old, barring a day.

At this critical moment the bride gave a third sneeze, and Billy roared out with all his might, "God save us!" Whether this exclamation resulted from his soliloquy, or from the mere force of habit, he never could tell exactly himself; but no sooner was it uttered than the little man, his face glowing with rage and disappointment, sprung from the beam on which he had perched himself, and shrieking out in the shrill voice of a cracked bagpipe, "I discharge you from my service, Billy Mac Daniel — take *that* for your wages," gave poor Billy a most furious kick in the back, which sent his unfortunate servant sprawling upon his face and hands right in the middle of the supper table.

If Billy was astonished, how much more so was every one of the company into which he was thrown with so little ceremony. But when they heard his story, Father Cooney laid down his knife and fork, and married the young couple out of hand with all speed; and Billy Mac Daniel danced the Rinka at their wedding, and plenty he did drink at it too, which was what he thought more of than dancing.

13: THE WITCHES' EXCURSION

Shemus Rua (Red James) awakened from his sleep one night by noises in his kitchen. Stealing to the door, he saw half-a-dozen old women sitting round the fire, jesting and laughing, his old housekeeper, Madge, quite frisky and gay, helping her sister crones to cheering glasses of punch. He began to admire the impudence and imprudence of Madge, displayed in the invitation and the riot, but recollected on the instant her officiousness in urging him to take a comfortable posset, which she had brought to his bedside just before he fell asleep. Had he drunk it, he would have been just now deaf to the witches' glee. He heard and saw them drink his health in such a mocking style as nearly to tempt him to charge them, besom in hand, but he restrained himself.

The jug being emptied, one of them cried out, "Is it time to be gone?" and at the same moment, putting on a red cap, she added —

> "By yarrow and rue,
> And my red cap too,
> Hie over to England."

Making use of a twig which she held in her hand as a steed, she gracefully soared up the chimney, and was rapidly followed by the rest. But when it came to the housekeeper, Shemus interposed. "By your leave, ma'am," said he, snatching twig and cap. "Ah, you desateful ould crocodile! If I find you here on my return, there'll be wigs on the green —

> "By yarrow and rue,
> And my red cap too,
> Hie over to England."

The words were not out of his mouth when he was soaring above the ridge pole, and swiftly ploughing the air. He was careful to speak no word (being somewhat conversant with witchlore), as the result would be a tumble, and the immediate return of the expedition.

In a very short time they had crossed the Wicklow hills, the Irish Sea, and the Welsh mountains, and were charging, at whirlwind speed, the hall door of a castle. Shemus, only for the company in which he found himself, would have cried out for pardon, expecting to be *mummy* against the hard oak door in a moment; but, all bewildered, he found himself passing through the keyhole, along a passage, down a flight of steps, and through a cellar door keyhole before he could form any clear idea of his situation.

Waking to the full consciousness of his position, he found himself sitting on a stallion, plenty of lights glimmering round, and he and his companions, with full tumblers of frothing wine in hand, hobnobbing and drinking healths as jovially and recklessly as if the liquor was honestly come by, and they were sitting in Shemus's own kitchen. The red cap has assimilated Shemus's nature for the time being to that of his unholy companions. The heady liquors soon got into their brains, and a period of un-consciousness succeeded the ecstasy, the headache, the turning round of the barrels, and the "scattered sight" of poor Shemus.

He woke up under the impression of being roughly seized, and shaken, and dragged upstairs, and subjected to a disagreeable examination by the lord of the castle, in his state parlour. There was much derision among the whole company, gentle and simple,

on hearing Shemus's explanation, and, as the thing occurred in the dark ages, the unlucky Leinster man was sentenced to be hung as soon as the gallows could be prepared for the occasion.

The poor Hibernian was in the cart proceeding on his last journey, with a label on his back, and another on his breast, announcing him as the remorseless villain who for the last month had been draining the casks in my lord's vault every night. He was surprised to hear himself addressed by his name, and in his native tongue, by an old woman in the crowd.

"Ach, Shemus, alanna! is it going to die you are in a strange place without your *cappen d'yarrag?*"

These words infused hope and courage into the poor victim's heart. He turned to the lord and humbly asked leave to die in his red cap, which he supposed had dropped from his head in the vault. A servant was sent for the headpiece, and Shemus felt lively hope warming his heart while placing it on his head. On the platform he was graciously allowed to address the spectators, which he proceeded to do in the usual formula composed for the benefit of flying stationers –

"Good people all, a warning take by me;" but when he had finished the line, "My parents reared me tenderly," he unexpectedly added –

> "By yarrow and rue,
> And my red cap too,
> Hie over to England."

The disappointed spectators saw him shoot up obliquely through the air in the style of a sky-rocket that had missed its aim.

14: THE MAN WHO NEVER KNEW FEAR

There was once a lady, and she had two sons whose names were Louras (Lawrence) and Carrol. From the day that Lawrence was born nothing ever made him afraid, but Carrol would never go outside the door from the time the darkness of the night began.

It was the custom at that time when a person died for people to watch the dead person's grave in turn, one after another; for there used to be destroyers going about stealing the corpses.

When the mother of Carrol and Lawrence died, Carrol said to Lawrence—

"You say that nothing ever made you afraid yet, but I'll make a bet with you that you haven't courage to watch your mother's tomb tonight."

"I'll make a bet with you that I have," said Lawrence.

When the darkness of the night was coming, Lawrence put on his sword and went to the burying ground. He sat down on a tombstone near his mother's grave till it was far in the night and sleep was coming upon him. Then he saw a big black thing coming to him, and when it came near him he saw that it was a head without a body that was in it. He drew the sword to give it a blow if it should come any nearer, but it didn't come. Lawrence remained looking at it until the light of the day was coming, then the head-without-body went, and Lawrence came home.

Carrol asked him, did he see anything in the graveyard.

"I did," said Lawrence, "and my mother's body would be gone, but that I was guarding it."

"Was it dead or alive, the person you saw?" said Carrol.

"I don't know was it dead or alive," said Lawrence; "there was nothing in it but a head without a body."

"Weren't you afraid?" says Carrol.

"Indeed I wasn't," said Lawrence; "don't you know that nothing in the world ever put fear on me."

"I'll bet again with you that you haven't the courage to watch tonight again," says Carrol.

"I would make that bet with you," said Lawrence, "but that there is a night's sleep wanting to me. Go yourself tonight."

"I wouldn't go to the graveyard tonight if I were to get the riches of the world," says Carrol.

"Unless you go your mother's body will be gone in the morning," says Lawrence.

"If only you watch tonight and tomorrow night, I never will ask of you to do a turn of work as long as you will be alive," said Carrol, "but I think there is fear on you."

"To show you that there's no fear on me," said Lawrence, "I will watch."

He went to sleep, and when the evening came he rose up, put on his sword, and went to the graveyard. He sat on a tombstone near his mother's grave. About the middle of the night he heard a great sound coming. A big black thing came as far as the grave and began rooting up the clay. Lawrence drew back his sword, and with one blow he made two halves of the big black thing, and with the second blow he made two halves of each half, and he saw it no more.

Lawrence went home in the morning, and Carrol asked him did he see anything.

"I did," said Lawrence, "and only that I was there my mother's

body would be gone."

"Is it the head–without–body that came again?" said Carrol.

"It was not, but a big black thing, and it was digging up my mother's grave until I made two halves of it."

Lawrence slept that day, and when the evening came he rose up, and put on his sword, and went to the churchyard. He sat down on a tombstone until it was the middle of the night. Then he saw a thing as white as snow and as hateful as sin; it had a man's head on it, and teeth as long as a flax–carder. Lawrence drew back the sword and was going to deal it a blow, when it said:

"Hold your hand; you have saved your mother's body, and there is not a man in Ireland as brave as you. There is great riches waiting for you if you go looking for it."

Lawrence went home, and Carrol asked him did he see anything.

"I did," said Lawrence, "and but that I was there my mother's body would be gone, but there's no fear of it now."

In the morning, the day on the morrow, Lawrence said to Carrol —

"Give me my share of money, and I'll go on a journey, until I have a look round the country."

Carrol gave him the money, and he went walking. He went on until he came to a large town. He went into the house of a baker to get bread. The baker began talking to him, and asked him how far he was going.

"I am going looking for something that will put fear on me," said Lawrence.

"Have you much money?" said the baker.

"I have a half-hundred pounds," said Lawrence.

"I'll bet another half-hundred with you that there will be fear on you if you go to the place that I'll bid you," says the baker.

"I'll take your bet," said Lawrence, "if only the place is not too far away from me."

"It's not a mile from the place where you're standing," said the baker. "Wait here till the night comes, and then go to the graveyard, and as a sign that you were in it, bring me the goblet that is upon the altar of the old church that is in the graveyard."

When the baker made the bet he was certain that he would win, for there was a ghost in the churchyard, and nobody went into it for forty years before that whom he did not kill.

When the darkness of the night came, Lawrence put on his sword and went to the burying ground. He came to the door of the churchyard and struck it with his sword. The door opened, and there came out a great black ram, and two horns on him as long as flails. Lawrence gave him a blow, and he went out of sight, leaving him up to the ankles in blood. Lawrence went into the old church, got the goblet, came back to the baker's house, gave him the goblet, and got the bet. Then the baker asked him did he see anything in the churchyard.

"I saw a big black ram with long horns on him," said Lawrence, "and I gave him a blow which drew as much blood out of him as would swim a boat; sure he must be dead by this time."

In the morning, the day on the morrow, the baker and a lot of people went to the graveyard and they saw the blood of the black ram at the door. They went to the priest and told him that the black ram was banished out of the churchyard. The priest did not believe them, because the churchyard was shut up forty years before that on account of the ghost that was in it, and neither priest nor friar could banish him. The priest came with them to the door of the churchyard, and when he saw the blood he took courage and sent for Lawrence, and heard the story from his own mouth. Then he sent for his blessing materials, and desired the people to come in till he read mass for them. The priest went in, and Lawrence and the people after him, and he read mass without the big black ram coming as he used to do. The priest was greatly rejoiced, and gave Lawrence another fifty pounds.

On the morning of the next day Lawrence went on his way. He travelled the whole day without seeing a house. About the hour of midnight he came to a great lonely valley, and he saw a large gathering of people looking at two men hurling. Lawrence stood looking at them, as there was a bright light from the moon. It was the good people that were in it, and it was not long until one of them struck a blow on the ball and sent it into Lawrence's breast. He put his hand in after the ball to draw it out, and what was there in it but the head of a man. When Lawrence got hold of it, it began screeching, and at last it asked Lawrence —

"Are you not afraid?"

"Indeed I am not," said Lawrence, and no sooner was the

word spoken than both head and people disappeared, and he was left in the glen alone by himself.

He journeyed until he came to another town, and when he ate and drank enough, he went out on the road, and was walking until he came to a great house on the side of the road. As the night was closing in, he went in to try if he could get lodging. There was a young man at the door who said to him –

"How far are you going, or what are you in search of?"

"I do not know how far I am going, but I am in search of something that will put fear on me," said Lawrence.

"You have not far to go, then," said the young man; "if you stop in that big house on the other side of the road there will be fear put on you before morning, and I'll give you twenty pounds into the bargain."

"I'll stop in it," said Lawrence.

The young man went with him, opened the door, and brought him into a large room in the bottom of the house, and said to him, "Put down fire for yourself and I'll send you plenty to eat and drink." He put down a fire for himself, and there came a girl to him and brought him everything that he wanted.

He went on very well, until the hour of midnight came, and then he heard a great sound over his head, and it was not long until a stallion and a bull came in and commenced to fight. Lawrence never put to them nor from them, and when they were tired fighting they went out. Lawrence went to sleep, and he never awoke until the young man came in in the morning, and he was surprised when he saw Lawrence alive. He asked him had he seen anything.

"I saw a stallion and a bull fighting hard for about two hours," said Lawrence.

"And weren't you afraid?" said the young man.

"I was not," says Lawrence.

"If you wait tonight again, I'll give you another twenty

pounds," says the young man.

"I'll wait, and welcome," says Lawrence.

The second night, about ten o'clock, Lawrence was going to sleep, when two black rams came in and began fighting hard. Lawrence neither put to them nor from them, and when twelve o'clock struck they went out. The young man came in the morning and asked him did he see anything last night.

"I saw two black rams fighting," said Lawrence.

"Were you afraid at all?" said the young man.

"I was not," said Lawrence.

"Wait tonight, and I'll give you another twenty pounds," says the young man.

"All right," says Lawrence.

The third night he was falling asleep, when there came in a grey old man and said to him –

"You are the best hero in Ireland; I died twenty years ago, and all that time I have been in search of a man like you. Come with me now till I show you your riches; I told you when you were watching your mother's grave that there was great riches waiting for you."

He took Lawrence to a chamber underground, and showed him a large pot filled with gold, and said to him —

"You will have all that if you give twenty pounds to Mary Kerrigan the widow and get her forgiveness for me for a wrong I did her. Then buy this house, marry my daughter, and you will be happy and rich as long as you live."

The next morning the young man came to Lawrence and asked him did he see anything last night.

"I did," said Lawrence, "and it's certain that there will be a ghost always in it, but nothing in the world would frighten me; I'll buy the house and the land round it, if you like."

"I'll ask no price for the house, but I won't part with the land under a thousand pounds, and I'm sure you haven't that much."

"I have more than would buy all the land and all the herds you have," said Lawrence.

When the young man heard that Lawrence was so rich, he invited him to come to dinner. Lawrence went with him, and when the dead man's daughter saw him she fell in love with him.

Lawrence went to the house of Mary Kerrigan and gave her twenty pounds, and got her forgiveness for the dead man. Then he married the young man's sister and spent a happy life. He died as he lived, without there being fear on him.

15: THE HORNED WOMEN

A rich woman sat up late one night carding and preparing wool, while all the family and servants were asleep. Suddenly a knock was given at the door, and a voice called — "Open! open!"

"Who is there?" said the woman of the house.

"I am the Witch of the one Horn," was answered.

The mistress, supposing that one of her neighbours had called and required assistance, opened the door, and a woman entered, having in her hand a pair of wool carders, and bearing a horn on her forehead, as if growing there. She sat down by the fire in silence, and began to card the wool with violent haste. Suddenly she paused, and said aloud: "Where are the women? they delay too long."

Then a second knock came to the door, and a voice called as before, "Open! open!"

The mistress felt herself constrained to rise and open to the call, and immediately a second witch entered, having two horns on her forehead, and in her hand a wheel for spinning wool.

"Give me place," she said, "I am the Witch of the two Horns," and she began to spin as quick as lightning.

And so the knocks went on, and the call was heard, and the witches entered, until at last twelve women sat round the fire — the first with one horn, the last with twelve horns.

And they carded the thread, and turned their spinning wheels, and wound and wove.

All singing together an ancient rhyme, but no word did they speak to the mistress of the house. Strange to hear, and frightful to look upon, were these twelve women, with their horns and their wheels; and the mistress felt near to death, and she tried to rise that she might call for help, but she could not move, nor could she utter a word or a cry, for the spell of the witches was upon her.

Then one of them called to her in Irish, and said –

"Rise, woman, and make us a cake." Then the mistress searched for a vessel to bring water from the well that she might mix the meal and make the cake, but she could find none.

And they said to her, "Take a sieve and bring water in it."

And she took the sieve and went to the well; but the water poured from it, and she could fetch none for the cake, and she sat down by the well and wept.

Then a voice came by her and said, "Take yellow clay and moss, and bind them together, and plaster the sieve so that it will hold."

This she did, and the sieve held water for the cake; and the voice said again –

"Return, and when thou comest to the north angle of the house, cry aloud three times and say, 'The mountain of the Fenian women and the sky over it is all on fire.'"

And she did so.

When the witches inside heard the call, a great and terrible cry broke from their lips, and they rushed forth with wild lamentations and shrieks, and fled away to Slievenamon,* where was their chief abode. But the Spirit of the Well bade the mistress of the house to enter and prepare her home against the enchantments of witches if they returned again.

And first, to break their spells, she sprinkled the water in

* *Sliábh-na-mban* – i.e., mountains of the women.

100

which she had washed her child's feet (the feet-water) outside the door on the threshold; secondly, she took the cake which the witches had made in her absence of meal mixed with the blood drawn from the sleeping family, and she broke the cake in bits, and placed a bit in the mouth of each sleeper, and they were restored; and she took the cloth they had woven and placed it half in and half out of the chest with the padlock; and lastly, she secured the door with a great crossbeam fastened in the jambs, so that they could not enter, and having done these things she waited.

Not long were the witches in coming back, and they raged and called for vengeance.

"Open, open!" they screamed, "open, feet-water!"

"I cannot," said the feet-water, "I am scattered on the ground, and my path is down to the Lough."

"Open, open, wood and trees and beam!" they cried to the door.

"I cannot," said the door, "for the beam is fixed in the jambs and I have no power to move."

"Open, open, cake that we have made and mingled with blood!" they cried again.

"I cannot," said the cake, "for I am broken and bruised, and my blood is on the lips of the sleeping children."

Then the witches rushed through the air with great cries, and fled back to Slievenamon, uttering strange curses on the Spirit of the Well, who had wished their ruin; but the woman and the house were left in peace, and a mantle dropped by one of the witches in her flight was kept hung up by the mistress as a sign of the night's awful contest; and this mantle was in possession of the same family from generation to generation for five hundred years after.

15: DANIEL O'ROURKE

People may have heard of the renowned adventures of Daniel O'Rourke, but how few are there who know that the cause of all his perils, above and below, was neither more nor less than having slept under the walls of the Pooka's tower.

I knew the man well. He lived at the bottom of Hungry Hill, just at the right-hand side of the road as you go towards Bantry. An old man was he, at the time he told me the story, with grey hair and a red nose; and it was on the 25th of June 1813 that I heard it from his own lips, as he sat smoking his pipe under the old poplar tree, on as fine an evening as ever shone from the sky. I was going to visit the caves in Dursey Island, having spent the morning at Glengariff.

"I am often *axed* to tell it, sir," said he, "so that this is not the first time. The master's son, you see, had come from beyond foreign parts in France and Spain, as young gentlemen used to go before Buonaparte or any such was heard of; and sure enough there was a dinner given to all the people on the ground, gentle and simple, high and low, rich and poor. The *ould* gentlemen were the gentlemen after all, saving your honour's presence. They'd swear at a body a little, to be sure, and, maybe, give one a cut of a whip now and then, but we were no losers by it in the end; and they were so easy and civil, and kept such rattling houses, and thousands of welcomes; and there was no grinding for rent, and there was hardly a tenant on the estate that did not taste of his landlord's bounty often and often in a year; but now it's another thing. No matter for that, sir, for I'd better be telling you my story.

"Well, we had everything of the best, and plenty of it; and we ate, and we drank, and we danced, and the young master by the same token danced with Peggy Barry, from the Bohereen – a lovely young couple they were, though they are both low enough now. To make a long story short, I got, as a body may say, the same thing as tipsy almost, for I can't remember ever at all, no ways, how it was I left the place; only I did leave it, that's certain.

"Well, I thought, for all that, in myself, I'd just step to Molly Cronohan's, the fairy woman, to speak a word about the bracket heifer that was bewitched; and so as I was crossing the stepping-stones of the ford of Ballyashenogh, and was looking up at the stars and blessing myself – for why? it was Lady-day – I missed my foot, and souse I fell into the water. 'Death alive!' thought I, 'I'll be drowned now!' However, I began swimming, swimming away for the dear life, till I got ashore, somehow or other, but never the one of me can tell how, upon a *dissolute* island.

"I wandered and wandered about there, without knowing where I wandered, until at last I got into a big bog. The moon was shining as bright as day, or your fair lady's eyes, sir (with your pardon for mentioning her), and I looked east and west, and north and south, and every way, and nothing did I see but bog, bog, bog – I could never find out how I got into it; and my heart grew cold with fear, for sure and certain I was that it would be my *berrin* place.

"So I sat down upon a stone which, as good luck would have it, was close by me, and I began to scratch my head, and sing the *Ullagone* – when all of a sudden the moon grew black, and I looked up, and saw something for all the world as if it was moving down

104

between me and it, and I could not tell what it was. Down it came with a pounce, and looked at me full in the face; and what was it but an eagle? as fine a one as ever flew from the kingdom of Kerry.

"So he looked at me in the face, and says he to me, 'Daniel O'Rourke,' says he, 'how do you do?'

" 'Very well, I thank you, sir,' says I; 'I hope you're well;' wondering out of my senses all the time how an eagle came to speak like a Christian.

" 'What brings you here, Dan,' says he.

" 'Nothing at all, sir,' says I; 'only I wish I was safe home again.'

" 'Is it out of the island you want to go, Dan?' says he.

" ' 'Tis, sir,' says I: so I up and told him how I had taken a drop too much, and fell into the water; how I swam to the island; and how I got into the bog and did not know my way out of it.

" 'Dan,' says he, after a minute's thought, 'though it is very improper for you to get drunk on Lady-day, yet as you are a decent man sober, who 'tends mass well, and never fling stones at me or mine, nor cries out after us in the fields – my life for yours,' says he; 'so get up on my back, and grip me well for fear you'd fall off, an I'll fly you out of the bog.'

" 'I am afraid,' says I, 'your honour's making game of me; for who ever heard of riding a horseback on an eagle before?'

" ' 'Pon the honour of a gentleman,' says he, putting his right foot on his breast, 'I am quite in earnest: and so now either take my offer or starve in the bog — besides, I see that your weight is sinking the stone.'

"It was true enough as he said, for I found the stone every minute going from under me. I had no choice; so thinks I to myself, faint heart never won fair lady, and this is fair persuadance.

" 'I thank your honour,' says I 'for the loan of your civility; and I'll take your kind offer.' I therefore mounted upon the back of the eagle, and held him tight enough by the throat, and up he flew in the air like a lark. Little I knew the trick he was going to serve me. Up — up — up, God knows how far up he flew.

" 'Why then,' said I to him — thinking he did not know the right road home — very civilly, because why? I was in his power entirely 'sir,' says I, 'please your honour's glory, and with humble submission to your better judgement, if you'd fly down a bit, you're now just over my cabin, and I could be put down there, and many thanks to your worship.'

" '*Arrah*, Dan,' said he, 'do you think me a fool? Look down in the next field, and don't you see two men and a gun? By my word it would be no joke to be shot this way, to oblige a drunken blackguard that I picked up off of a *could* stone in a bog.'

" 'Bother you,' said I to myself, but I did not speak out, for where was the use? Well, sir, up he kept, flying, flying, and I asking him every minute to fly down, and all to no use.

" 'Where in the world are you going, sir?' says I to him.

" 'Hold your tongue, Dan,' says he: 'mind your own business, and don't be interfering with the business of other people.'

" 'Faith, this is my business I think,' says I.

" 'Be quiet, Dan,' says he: so I said no more.

"At last where should we come to, but to the moon itself. Now

you can't see it from this, but there is, or there was in my time, a reaping-hook sticking out of the side of the moon, this way (drawing the figure thus ☞ on the ground with the end of his stick).

" 'Dan,' said the eagle, 'I'm tired with this long fly; I had no notion 'twas so far.'

" 'And my lord, sir,' said I, 'who in the world *axed* you to fly so far — was it I? did not I beg and pray and beseech you to stop half an hour ago?'

" 'There's no use talking, Dan,' said he; 'I'm tired bad enough, so you must get off, and sit down on the moon until I rest myself.'

" 'Is it sit down on the moon?' said I; 'is it upon that little round thing, then? why, then, sure I'd fall off in a minute, and be *kilt* and spilt, and smashed all to bits; you are a vile deceiver — so you are.'

" 'Not at all, Dan,' said he; 'you can catch fast hold of the reaping-hook that's sticking out of the side of the moon, and 'twill keep you up.'

" 'I won't then,' said I.

" 'Maybe not,' said he, quite quiet. 'If you don't, my man, I shall just give you a shake, and one slap of my wing, and send you down to the ground, where every bone in your body will be smashed as small as a drop of dew on a cabbage in the morning.'

" 'Why, then, I'm in a fine way,' said I to myself, 'ever to have come along with the likes of you,' and so giving him a hearty curse in Irish, for fear he'd know what I said, I got off his back with a heavy heart, took hold of the reaping-hook, and sat down upon the moon, and a mighty cold seat it was, I can tell you that.

"When he had me there fairly landed, he turned about on me, and said, 'Good morning to you, Daniel O'Rourke,' said he; 'I think I've nicked you fairly now. You robbed my nest last year' ('twas true enough for him, but how he found out is hard to say), 'and in return you are freely welcome to cool your heels dangling upon the moon like a cockthrow.'

" 'Is that all, and is this the way you leave me, you brute, you?' says I. 'You ugly unnatural *baste,* and is this the way you serve me at last? Bad luck to yourself, with your hook'd nose, and to all your breed, you blackguard.'

" 'Twas all to no manner of use; he spread out his great big wings, burst out a laughing, and flew away like lightning. I bawled after him to stop; but I might have called and bawled for ever, without his minding me. Away he went, and I never saw him from that day to this — sorrow fly away with him!

"You may be sure I was in a disconsolate condition, and kept roaring out for the bare grief, when all at once a door opened right in the middle of the moon, creaking on its hinges as if it had not been opened for a month before, I suppose they never thought of greasing 'em, and out there walks — who do you think but the man in the moon himself? I knew him by his bush.

" 'Good morrow to you, Daniel O'Rourke,' said he; 'how do you do?'

" 'Very well, thank your honour,' said I. 'I hope your honour's well.'

" 'What brought you here, Dan?' said he.

"So I told him how I was a little overtaken in liquor at the master's, and how I was cast on a *dissolute* island, and how I lost my way in the bog, and how the thief of an eagle promised to fly me out of it, and how, instead of that, he had fled me up to the moon.

" 'Dan,' said the man in the moon, taking a pinch of snuff when I was done, 'you must not stay here.'

" 'Indeed, sir,' says I, ' 'tis much against my will I'm here at all; but how am I to go back?'

" 'That's your business,' said he; 'Dan, mine is to tell you that here you must not stay; so be off in less than no time.'

" 'I'm doing no harm,' says I, 'only holding on hard by the reaping-hook, lest I fall off.'

" 'That's what you must not do, Dan,' says he.

" 'Pray, sir,' says I, 'may I ask how many you are in family, that you would not give a poor traveller lodging: I'm sure 'tis not often you're troubled with strangers coming to see you, for 'tis a long way.'

" 'I'm by myself, Dan,' says he; 'but you'd better let go the reaping-hook.'

" 'Faith, and with your leave,' says I, 'I'll not let go the grip, and the more you bids me, the more I won't let go; – so I will.'

" 'You had better, Dan,' says he again.

" 'Why, then, my little fellow,' says I, taking the whole weight of him with my eye from head to foot, 'there are two words to that bargain; and I'll not budge, but you may if you like.'

" 'We'll see how that is to be,' says he; and back he went, giving the door such a great bang after him (for it was plain he was huffed) that I thought the moon and all would fall down with it.

"Well, I was preparing myself to try strength with him, when back again he comes, with the kitchen cleaver in his hand, and, without saying a word, he gives two bangs to the handle of the reaping-hook that was keeping me up, and *whap*! it came in two.

" 'Good morning to you, Dan,' says the spiteful little old black-guard, when he saw me cleanly falling down with a bit of the handle in my hand; 'I thank you for your visit, and fair weather after you, Daniel.'

"I had not time to make any answer to him, for I was tumbling over and over, and rolling and rolling, at the rate of a fox-hunt. 'God help me!' says I, 'but this is a pretty pickle for a decent man to be seen in at this time of night: I am now sold fairly.'

"The word was not out of my mouth when whiz! what should fly by close to my ear but a flock of wild geese, all the way from my own bog of Ballyasheenogh, else how should they know *me* ? The *ould* gander, who was their general, turning about his head, cried out to me, 'Is that you, Dan?'

" 'The same,' said I, not a bit daunted now at what he said, for I was by this time used to all kinds of *bedevilment*, and, besides, I knew him of *ould*.

" 'Good morrow to you,' says he, 'Daniel O'Rourke; how are you in health this morning?'

" 'Very well, sir,' says I, 'I thank you kindly,' drawing my breath, for I was mightily in want of some. 'I hope your honour's the same.'

" 'I think 'tis falling you are, Daniel,' says he.

" 'You may say that, sir,' says I.

" 'And where are you going all the way so fast?' said the gander.

" So I told him how I had taken the drop, and how I came on the island, and how I lost my way in the bog, and how the thief of an eagle flew me up to the moon, and how the man in the moon turned me out.

" 'Dan,' said he, 'I'll save you: put out your hand and catch me by the leg, and I'll fly you home.'

" 'Sweet is your hand in a pitcher of honey, my jewel,' says I, though all the time I thought within myself that I don't much trust you; but there was no help, so I caught the gander by the leg, and away I and the other geese flew after him as fast as hops.

"We flew, and we flew, and we flew, until we came right over the wide ocean. I knew it well, for I saw Cape Clear to my right hand, sticking up out of the water.

" 'Ah, my lord,' said I to the goose, for I thought it best to

keep a civil tongue on my head anyway, 'fly to land if you please.'

" 'It is impossible, you see, Dan,' said he, 'for a while, because you see we are going to Arabia.'

" 'To Arabia!' said I; 'that's surely some place in foreign parts, far away. Oh! Mr Goose: why then, to be sure, I'm a man to be pitied among you.'

" 'Whist, whist, you fool,' said he, 'hold your tongue; I tell you Arabia is a very decent sort of place, as like West Carbery as one egg is like another, only there is a little more sand there.'

"Just as we were talking, a ship hove in sight, scudding so beautiful before the wind.

" 'Ah! then, sir,' said I, 'will you drop me on the ship, if you please?'

" 'We are not fair over it,' said he; 'if I dropped you now you would go splash into the sea.'

" 'I would not,' says I; 'I know better than that, for it is just clean under us, so let me drop now at once.'

" 'If you must, you must,' said he; 'there, take your own way;' and he opened his claw, and faith he was right — sure enough I came down plump into the very bottom of the salt sea! Down to

113

the very bottom I went, and I gave myself up then for ever, when a whale walked up to me, scratching himself after his night's sleep, and he looked me full in the face, and never the word did he say, but lifting up his tail, he splashed me all over again with the cold salt water till there wasn't a dry stitch upon my whole carcass! and I heard somebody saying — 'twas a voice I knew, too — 'Get up you drunken brute, off o' that;' and with that I woke up, and there was Judy with a tub full of water, which she was splashing all over me — for, rest her soul! though she was a good wife, she never could bear to see me in drink, and had a bitter hand of her own.

" 'Get up,' said she again: 'and of all places in the parish would no place *sarve* your turn to lie down upon but under the *ould* walls of Carrigapooka? an uneasy resting I am sure you had of it.'

"And sure enough I had: for I was fairly bothered out of my senses with eagles, and men of the moons, and flying ganders, and whales, driving me through bogs, and up to the moon, and down to the bottom of the green ocean. If I was in drink ten times over, long would it be before I'd lie down in the same spot again, I know that."

17: THE SOUL CAGES

Jack Dogherty lived on the coast of the county Clare. Jack was a fisherman, as his father and grandfather before him had been. Like them, too, he lived all alone (but for the wife), and just in the same spot. People used to wonder why the Dogherty family were so fond of that wild situation, so far away from all human kind, and in the midst of huge shattered rocks, with nothing but the wide ocean to look upon. But they had their own good reasons for it.

The place was just the only spot on that part of the coast where anybody could well live. There was a neat little creek, where a boat might lie as snug as a puffin in her nest, and out from this creek a ledge of sunken rocks ran into the sea. Now when the Atlantic, according to custom, was raging with a storm, and a good westerly wind was blowing strong on the coast, many a richly-laden ship went to pieces on these rocks; and then the fine bales of cotton and tobacco, and such like things, and the pipes of wine and the puncheons of rum, and the casks of brandy, and the kegs of Hollands that used to come ashore! Dunbeg Bay was just like a little estate to the Dohertys.

Not but they were kind and humane to a distressed sailor, if ever one had the good luck to get to land; and many a time indeed did Jack put out in his little *corragh* (which, though not quite equal to honest Andrew Hennessy's canvas lifeboat would breast the billows like any gannet), to lend a hand towards bringing off the crew from a wreck. But when the ship had gone to pieces, and the crew were all lost, who would blame Jack for picking up all he could find?

"And who is the worse of it?" said he. "For as to the king, God bless him! everybody knows he's rich enough already without getting what's floating in the sea."

Jack, though such a hermit, was a good-natured, jolly fellow. No other, sure, could ever have coaxed Biddy Mahony to quit her father's snug and warm house in the middle of the town of Ennis, and to go so many miles off to live among the rocks, with the seals and seagulls for next-door neighbours. But Biddy knew that Jack was the man for a woman who wished to be comfortable and happy; for to say nothing of the fish, Jack had the supplying of half the gentlemen's houses of the country with the *Godsends* that came into the bay. And she was right in her choice; for no woman ate, drank, or slept better, or made a prouder appearance at chapel on Sundays, than Mrs Dogherty.

Many a strange sight, it may well be supposed, did Jack see, and many a strange sound did he hear, but nothing daunted him. So far was he from being afraid of Merrows, or such beings, that the very first wish of his heart was to fairly meet with one. Jack had heard that they were mighty like Christians, and that luck had always come out of an acquaintance with them. Never, therefore, did he dimly discern the Merrows moving along the face of the waters in their robes of mist, but he made direct for them; and many a scolding did Biddy, in her own quiet way, bestow upon Jack for spending his whole day out at sea, and bringing home no fish. Little did poor Biddy know the fish Jack was after!

It was rather annoying to Jack that, though living in a place where the Merrows were as plenty as lobsters, he never could get a right view of one. What vexed him more was that both his father and grandfather had often and often seen them; and he even remembered hearing, when a child, how his grandfather, who

116

was the first of the family that had settled down at the creek, had been so intimate with a Merrow that, only for fear of vexing the priest, he would have had him stand for one of his children. This, however, Jack did not well know how to believe.

Fortune at length began to think that it was only right that Jack should know as much as his father and grandfather did. Accordingly, one day when he had strolled a little farther than usual along the coast to the northward, just as he turned a point, he saw something, like to nothing he had ever seen before, perched upon a rock at a little distance out to sea. It looked green in the body, as well as he could discern at that distance, and he would have sworn, only the thing was impossible, that it had a cocked hat in its hand. Jack stood for a good half-hour straining his eyes, and wondering at it, and all the time the thing did not stir hand or foot. At last Jack's patience was quite worn out, and he gave a loud whistle and a hail, when the Merrow (for such it was) started up, put the cocked hat on its head, and dived down, head foremost, from the rock.

Jack's curiosity was now excited, and he constantly directed his steps towards the point; still he could never get a glimpse of the sea-gentleman with the cocked hat; and with thinking and thinking about the matter, he began at last to fancy he had been only dreaming. One very rough day, however, when the sea was running mountains high, Jack Dogherty determined to give a look at the Merrow's rock (for he had always chosen a fine day before), and then he saw the strange thing cutting capers upon the top of the rock, and then diving down, and then coming up, and then diving down again.

Jack had now only to choose his time (that is, a good blowing day), and he might see the man of the sea as often as he pleased. All this, however, did not satisfy him – "much will have more"; he wished now to get acquainted with the Merrow, and even in this he succeeded.

One tremendous blustering day, before he got to the point whence he had a view of the Merrow's rock, the storm came on so furiously that Jack was obliged to take shelter in one of the caves which are so numerous along the coast; and there, to his astonishment, he saw sitting before him a thing with green hair, long green teeth, a red nose, and pig's eyes. It had a fish's tail, legs with scales on them, and short arms like fins. It wore no clothes, but had the cocked hat under its arm, and seemed engaged thinking very seriously about something.

Jack, with all his courage, was a little daunted; but now or never, thought he; so up he went boldly to the cogitating fishman, took off his hat, and made his best bow.

"Your servant, sir," said Jack.

"Your servant, kindly, Jack Dogherty," answered the Merrow.

"To be sure, then, how well your honour knows my name!" said Jack.

"Is it I not know your name, Jack Dogherty? Why man, I knew your grandfather long before he was married to Judy Regan, your grandmother! Ah, Jack, Jack, I was fond of that grandfather of yours; he was a mighty worthy man in his time: I never met his match above or below, before or since, for sucking in a shellful of brandy. I hope, my boy," said the old fellow, with a merry twinkle in his eyes, "I hope you're his own grandson!"

"Never fear me for that," said Jack; "if my mother had only reared me on brandy, 'tis myself that would be a sucking infant to this hour!"

"Well, I like to hear you talk so manly; you and I must be better acquainted, if it were only for your grandfather's sake. But, Jack, that father of yours was not the thing! he had no head at all."

"I'm sure," said Jack, "since your honour lives down under the water, you must be obliged to drink a power to keep any heat in you in such a cruel, damp, *could* place. Well, I've often heard of Christians drinking like fishes; and might I be so bold as ask where you get the spirits?"

"Where do you get them yourself, Jack?" said the Merrow, twitching his red nose between his forefinger and thumb.

"Hubbubboo," cries Jack "now I see how it is; but I suppose, sir, your honour has got a fine dry cellar below to keep them in."

"Let me alone for the cellar," said the Merrow, with a knowing wink of his left eye.

"I'm sure," continued Jack, "it must be mighty well worth the looking at."

"You may say that, Jack," said the Merrow; "and if you meet me here next Monday, just at this time of the day, we will have a little more talk with one another about the matter."

Jack and the Merrow parted the best friends in the world. On

119

Monday they met, and Jack was not a little surprised to see that the Merrow had two cocked hats with him, one under each arm.

"Might I take the liberty to ask, sir," said Jack, "why your honour has brought the two hats with you today? You would not, sure, be going to give me one of them, to keep for the *curiosity* of the thing?"

"No, no, Jack," said he, "I don't get my hats so easily, to part with them that way; but I want you to come down and dine with me, and I brought you that hat to dive with."

"Lord bless and preserve us!" cried Jack, in amazement, "would you want me to go down to the bottom of the salt sea ocean? Sure, I'd be smothered and choked up with the water, to say nothing of being drowned! And what would poor Biddy do for me, and what would she say?"

"And what matter what she says, you *pinkeen*? Who cares for Biddy's squalling? It's long before your grandfather would have talked in that way. Many's the time he stuck that same hat on his head, and dived down boldly after me; and many's the snug bit of dinner and good shellful of brandy he and I have had together below, under the water."

"Is it really, sir, and no joke?" said Jack; "why, then, sorrow from me for ever and a day after, if I'll be a bit worse man nor my grandfather was! Here goes – but play me fair now. Here's neck or nothing!" cried Jack.

"That's your grandfather all over," said the old fellow; "so come along, then, and do as I do."

They both left the cave, walked into the sea, and then swam a piece until they got to the rock. The Merrow climbed to the top of it, and Jack followed him. On the far side it was as straight as the wall of a house, and the sea beneath looked so deep that Jack was almost cowed.

"Now, do you see, Jack," said the Merrow: "just put this hat on your head, and mind to keep your eyes wide open. Take

hold of my tail, and follow after me, and you'll see what you'll see."

In he dashed, and in dashed Jack after him boldly. They went and they went, and Jack thought they'd never stop going. Many a time did he wish himself sitting at home by the fireside with Biddy. Yet where was the use of wishing now, when he was so many miles, as he thought, below the waves of the Atlantic? Still he held hard by the Merrow's tail, slippery as it was; and, at last, to Jack's surprise, they got out of the water, and he actually found himself on dry land at the bottom of the sea. They landed just in front of a nice house that was slated very neatly with oyster shells! and the Merrow, turning about to face Jack, welcomed him down.

Jack could hardly speak, what with wonder, and what with being out of breath with travelling so fast through the water. He looked about him and could see no living things, barring crabs and lobsters, of which there were plenty walking leisurely about on the sand. Overhead was the sea like a sky, and the fishes like birds swimming about in it.

"Why don't you speak, man?" said the Merrow: "I dare say you had no notion that I had such a snug little concern here as this? Are you smothered, or choked, or drowned, or are you fretting after Biddy, eh?"

"Oh! not myself indeed," said Jack, showing his teeth with a good-humoured grin; "but who in the world would ever have thought of seeing such a thing?"

"Well, come along, and let's see what they've got for us to eat?"

Jack really was hungry, and it gave him no small pleasure to perceive a fine column of smoke rising from the chimney, announcing what was going on within. Into the house he followed the Merrow, and there he saw a good kitchen, right well provided with everything. There was a noble dresser, and plenty of pots and pans, with two young Merrows cooking. His host then led him into the room, which was furnished shabbily enough. Not a table or a chair was there in it; nothing but planks and logs of wood to sit on, and eat off. There was, however, a good fire blazing upon the hearth – a comfortable sight to Jack.

"Come now, and I'll show you where I keep – you know what," said the Merrow, with a sly look; and opening a little door, he led Jack into a fine cellar, well filled with pipes, and kegs, and hogsheads, and barrels.

"What do you say to that, Jack Dogherty? Eh! maybe a body can't live snug under the water?"

"Never the doubt of that," said Jack, with a convincing smack of his upper lip, that he really thought what he said.

They went back to the room, and found dinner laid. There was no tablecloth, to be sure – but what matter? It was not always Jack had one at home. The dinner would have been no discredit to the first house of the country on a fast day. The choicest of fish, and no wonder, was there. Turbots, and sturgeons, and soles, and lobsters, and oysters, and twenty other kinds, were on the planks at once, and plenty of the best of foreign spirits. The wines, the old fellow said, were too cold for his stomach.

Jack ate and drank till he could eat no more: then taking up a shell of brandy, "Here's to your honour's good health, sir," said he; "though, begging you pardon, it's mighty odd that as long as we've been acquainted I don't know your name yet."

"That's true, Jack," replied he; "I never thought of it before, but better late than never. My name's Coomara."

"And a mighty decent name it is," cried Jack, taking another shellfull: "here's to your good health, Coomara, and may ye live these fifty years to come!"

"Fifty years!" repeated Coomara; "I'm obliged to you, indeed! If you had said five hundred, it would have been something worth the wishing."

"By the laws, sir," cries Jack, "*youz* live to a powerful age here under the water! You knew my grandfather, and he's dead and gone better than these sixty years. I'm sure it must be a healthy place to live in."

"No doubt of it; but come, Jack, keep the liquor stirring."

Shell after shell did they empty, and to Jack's exceeding surprise, he found the drink never got into his head, owing, I suppose, to the sea being over them, which kept their noddles cool.

Old Coomara got exceedingly comfortable, and sang several songs; but Jack, if his life had depended on it, never could remember more than

> "Rum fum boodle boo,
>   Ripple dipple nitty dob;
> Dum doo doodle coo,
>   Raffle taffle chittibob!"

It was the chorus to one of them; and, to say the truth, nobody that I know has ever been able to pick any particular meaning out of it; but that, to be sure, is the case with many a song nowadays.

At length said he to Jack, "Now, my dear boy, if you follow

me, I'll show you my *curiosities*!" He opened a little door, and led Jack into a large room, where Jack saw a great many odds and ends that Coomara had picked up at one time or another. What chiefly took his attention, however, were things like lobster-pots ranged on the ground along the wall.

"Well, Jack, how do you like my *curiosities*?" said old Coo.

"Upon my *sowkins,** sir," said Jack, "they're mighty well worth the looking at; but might I make so bold as to ask what these things like lobster-pots are?"

"Oh! the Soul Cages, is it?"

"The what? sir!"

"These things here that I keep the souls in."

"*Arrah*! what souls, sir?" said Jack, in amazement; "sure the fish have no souls in them?"

"Oh! no," replied Coo, quite coolly, "that they have not; but these are the souls of drowned sailors."

"The Lord preserve us from all harm!" muttered Jack, "how in the world did you get them?"

"Easily enough: I've only, when I see a good storm coming on, to set a couple of dozen of these, and then, when the sailors are drowned and the souls get out of them under the water, the poor

* *sowkins,* diminutive of soul.

124

things are almost perished to death, not being used to the cold; so they make into my pots for shelter, and then I have them snug, and fetch them home, and is it not well for them, poor souls, to get such good quarters?"

Jack was so thunderstruck he did not know what to say, so he said nothing. They went back into the dining room, and had a little more brandy, which was excellent, and then, as Jack knew that it must be getting late, and as Biddy might be uneasy, he stood up, and said he thought it was time for him to be on the road.

"Just as you like, Jack," said Coo, "but take a *duc an durrus*† before you go; you've a cold journey before you."

Jack knew better manners than to refuse the parting glass.

"I wonder," said he, "will I be able to make out my way home?"

"What should ail you," said Coo, "when I'll show you the way?"

Out they went before the house, and Coomara took one of the cocked hats, and put it upon Jack's head the wrong way, and then lifted him up on his shoulder that he might launch him up into the water.

"Now," says he, giving him a heave, "you'll come up just in the same spot you came down in; and, Jack, mind and throw me back the hat."

He canted Jack off his shoulder, and up he shot like a bubble —
† *Recté, doech án dorrus* — door-drink or stirrup-cup.

whirr, whirr, whiz – away he went up through the water, till he came to the very rock he had jumped off where he found a landing-place, and then in he threw the hat, which sank like a stone.

The sun was just going down in the beautiful sky of a calm summer's evening. *Feascor* was seen dimly twinkling in the cloudless heaven, a solitary star, and the waves of the Atlantic flashed in a golden flood of light. So Jack, perceiving it was late, set off home; but when he got there, not a word did he say to Biddy of where he had spent his day.

The state of the poor souls cooped up in the lobster-pots gave Jack a great deal of trouble, and how to release them cost him a great deal of thought. He at first had a mind to speak to the priest about the matter. But what could the priest do, and what did Coo care for the priest? Besides, Coo was a good sort of an old fellow, and did not think he was doing any harm. Jack had a regard for him, too, and it also might not be much to his own credit if it were known that he used to go dine with Merrows. On the whole, he thought his best plan would be to ask Coo to dinner, and to make him drunk, if he was able, and then to take the hat and go down and turn up the pots. It was, first of all, necessary, however, to get Biddy out of the way; for Jack was prudent enough, as she was a woman, to wish to keep the thing secret from her.

Accordingly, Jack grew mighty pious all of a sudden, and said to Biddy that he thought it would be for the good of both their souls if she was to go and take her rounds at Saint John's Well, near Ennis. Biddy thought so too, and accordingly off she set one fine morning at day-dawn, giving Jack a strict charge to have an eye to the place. The coast being clear, away went Jack to the rock to give the appointed signal to Coomara, which was throwing a big stone into the water. Jack threw, and up sprang Coo!

"Good morning, Jack," said he; "what do you want with me?"

"Just nothing at all to speak about, sir," returned Jack, "only to come and take a bit of dinner with me, if I might make so free as to ask you, and sure I'm now after doing so."

"It's quite agreeable, Jack, I assure you; what's your hour?"

"Any time that's most convenient to you, sir — say one o'clock, that you may go home, if you wish, with the daylight."

"I'll be with you," said Coo, "never fear me."

Jack went home, and dressed a noble fish dinner, and got out plenty of his best foreign spirits, enough, for that matter, to make twenty men drunk. Just to the minute came Coo, with his cocked hat under his arm. Dinner was ready, they sat down, and ate and drank away manfully. Jack, thinking of the poor souls below in the pots, plied old Coo well with brandy, and encouraged him to sing, hoping to put him under the table, but poor Jack forgot that he had not the sea over his head to keep it cool. The brandy got into it, and did his business for him, and Coo reeled off home, leaving his entertainer as dumb as a haddock on a Good Friday.

Jack never woke till the next morning, and then he was in a sad way. " 'Tis to no use for me thinking to make that old Rapparee drunk," said Jack, "and how in this world can I help the poor souls out of the lobster-pots?" After ruminating nearly the whole day, a thought struck him. "I have it," says he, slapping his knee; "I'll be sworn that Coo never saw a drop of *poteen,* as old as he is, and that's the *thing* to settle him! Oh! then, is not it well that Biddy will not be home these two days yet; I can have another twist at him."

Jack asked Coo again, and Coo laughed at him for having no better head, telling him he'd never come up to his grandfather.

"Well, but try me again," said Jack, "and I'll be bail to drink you drunk and sober, and drunk again."

"Anything in my power," said Coo, "to oblige you."

At this dinner Jack took care to have his own liquor well watered, and to give the strongest brandy he had to Coo. At last says he, "Pray, sir, did you ever drink any poteen? — any real mountain dew?"

"No," says Coo; "what's that, and where does it come from?"

"Oh, that's a secret," said Jack, "but it's the right stuff – never believe me again, if 'tis not fifty times as good as brandy or rum either. Biddy's brother just sent me a present of a little drop, in exchange for some brandy, and as you're an old friend of the family, I kept it to treat you with."

"Well, let's see what sort of thing it is," said Coomara.

The *poteen* was the right sort. It was first-rate, and had the real smack upon it. Coo was delighted: he drank and he sang *Rum bum boodle boo* over and over again; and he laughed and he danced, till he fell on the floor fast asleep. Then Jack, who had taken good care to keep himself sober, snapped up the cocked hat – ran off to the rock – leaped, and soon arrived at Coo's habitation.

All was as still as a churchyard at midnight – not a Merrow, old or young, was there. In he went and turned up the pots, but nothing did he see, only he heard a sort of a little whistle or chirp as he raised each of them. At this he was surprised, till he recollected what the priests had often said, that nobody living could see the soul, no more than they could see the wind or the air. Having now done all that he could for them, he set the pots as they were before, and sent a blessing after the poor souls to speed them on their journey wherever they were going.

Jack now began to think of returning; he put the hat on, as was right, the wrong way; but when he got out he found the water so high over his head that he had no hopes of ever getting up into it, now that he had not old Coomara to give him a lift. He walked about looking for a ladder, but not one could he find, and not a rock was there in sight. At last he saw a spot where the sea hung rather lower than anywhere else, so he resolved to try there. Just as he came to it, a big cod happened to put down his tail. Jack made a jump and caught hold of it, and the cod, all in amazement, gave a bounce and pulled Jack up. The minute the hat touched the water away Jack was whisked, and up he shot like a cork, dragging the

128

poor cod, that he forgot to let go, up with him tail foremost. He got to the rock in no time and without a moment's delay hurried home, rejoicing in the good deed he had done.

But, meanwhile, there was fine work at home; for our friend Jack had hardly left the house on his soul-freeing expedition, when back came Biddy from her soul-saving one to the well. When she entered the house and saw the things lying *thrie-na-helah**on the table before her: "Here's a pretty job!" said she; "that blackguard of mine – what ill-luck I had ever to marry him! He has picked up some vagabond or other, while I was praying for the good of his soul, and they've been drinking all the *poteen* that my own brother gave him, and all the spirits, to be sure, that he was to have sold to his honour." Then hearing an outlandish kind of grunt, she looked down, and saw Coomara lying under the table. "The Blessed Virgin help me," shouted she, "if he has not made a real beast of himself! Well, well, I've often heard of a man making a beast of himself with drink! Oh hone, oh hone! – Jack, honey, what will I do with you, or what will I do without you? How can any decent woman ever think of living with a beast?"

With such like lamentations Biddy rushed out of the house, and was going she knew not where, when she heard the well-known voice of Jack singing a merry tune. Glad enough was Biddy to find him safe and sound, and not turned into a thing that was like neither fish nor flesh. Jack was obliged to tell her all, and Biddy, though she had half a mind to be angry with him for not telling her before, owned that he had done a great service to the poor souls.

Back they both went most lovingly to the house, and Jack wakened up Coomara; and, perceiving the old fellow to be rather dull, he bid him not to be cast down, for 'twas many a good man's case; said it all came of his not being used to the *poteen,* and recommended him, by way of cure, to swallow a hair of the dog that bit him. Coo, however, seemed to think he had had quite

* *Tri-na-cheile, literally through other* – i.e., higgledy-piggledy.

130

enough. He got up, quite out of sorts, and without having the manners to say one word in the way of civility, he sneaked off to cool himself by a jaunt through the salt water.

Coomara never missed the souls. He and Jack continued the best friends in the world, and no one, perhaps, ever equalled Jack for freeing souls from purgatory; for he contrived fifty excuses for getting into the house below the sea, unknown to the old fellow, and then turning up the pots and letting out the souls. It vexed him, to be sure, that he could never see them; but as he knew the thing to be impossible, he was obliged to be satisfied.

Their intercourse continued for several years. However, one morning, on Jack's throwing in a stone as usual, he got no answer. He flung another, and another, still there was no reply. He went away, and returned the following morning, but it was to no purpose. As he was without the hat, he could not go down to see what had become of old Coo, but his belief was, that the old man, or the old fish, or whatever he was, had either died, or had removed from that part of the country.

18: THE GIANT'S STAIRS

On the road between Passage and Cork there is an old mansion called Ronayne's Court. It may be easily known from the stack of chimneys and the gable-ends, which are to be seen, look at it which way you will. Here it was that Maurice Ronayne and his wife Margaret Gould kept house, as may be learned to this day from the great old chimney-piece, on which is carved their arms. They were a mighty worthy couple, and had but one son, who was called Philip, after no less a person than the King of Spain.

Immediately on his smelling the cold air of this world the child sneezed, which was naturally taken to be a good sign of his having a clear head; and the subsequent rapidity of his learning was truly amazing, for on the very first day a primer was put into his hands he tore out the A, B, C page and destroyed it, as a thing quite beneath his notice. No wonder, then, that both father and mother were proud of their heir, who gave such indisputable proofs of genius, or, as they called it in that part of the world, *"genus"*.

One morning, however, Master Phil, who was then just seven years old, was missing, and no one could tell what had become of him: servants were sent in all directions to seek him, on horse-back and on foot, but they returned without any tidings of the boy, whose disappearance altogether was most unaccountable. A large reward was offered, but it produced them no intelligence, and years

132

rolled away without Mr and Mrs Ronayne having obtained any satisfactory account of the fate of their lost child.

There lived at this time, near Carrigaline, one Robin Kelly, a blacksmith by trade. He was what is termed a handy man, and his abilities were held in much estimation by the lads and the lasses of the neighbourhood: for independent of shoeing horses, which he did to great perfection, and making plough-irons, he interpreted dreams for the young women, sang "Arthur O'Bradley" at their weddings, and was so good-natured a fellow at a christening, that he was gossip to half the country round.

Now it happened that Robin had a dream himself, and young Philip Ronayne appeared to him in it, at the dead hour of the night. Robin thought he saw the boy mounted upon a beautiful white horse, and that he told him how he was made a page to the giant Mahon MacMahon, who had carried him off, and who held his court in the hard heart of the rock. "The seven years — my time of service — are clean out, Robin," said he, "and if you release me this night I will be the making of you for ever after."

"And how will I know," said Robin — cunning enough, even in his sleep — "but this is all a dream?"

"Take that," said the boy, "for a token" — and at the word the white horse struck out with one of his hind legs, and gave poor Robin such a kick in the forehead that, thinking he was a dead man, he roared as loud as he could after his brains, and woke up, calling a thousand murders. He found himself in bed, but he had the mark of the blow, the regular print of a horse-shoe, upon his forehead as red as blood; and Robin Kelly, who never before found himself puzzled at the dream of any other person, did not know what to think of his own.

Robin was well acquainted with the Giant's Stairs — as, indeed, who is not that knows the harbour? They consist of great masses of rock, which, piled one above another, rise like a flight of steps from very deep water, against the bold cliff of Carrigmahon. Nor are they badly suited for stairs to those who have legs of sufficient length to stride over a moderate-sized house, or to enable them to clear the space of a mile in a hop, step, and jump. Both these feats the giant MacMahon was said to have performed in the days of Finnian glory; and the common tradition of the country placed his dwelling within the cliff up whose side the stairs led.

Such was the impression which the dream made on Robin, that he determined to put its truth to the test. It occurred to him, however, before setting out on his adventure, that a plough-iron may be no bad companion, as, from experience, he knew that it was an excellent knock-down argument, having on more occasions than one settled a little disagreement very quietly: so, putting one on his shoulder, off he marched, in the cool of the evening, through Glaun a Thowk (the Hawk's Glen) to Monkstown. Here an old gossip of his (Tom Clancey by name) lived, who on hearing Robin's dream, promised him the use of his skiff, and moreover, offered to assist in rowing it to the Giant's Stairs.

After supper, which was of the best, they embarked. It was a beautiful still night, and the little boat glided swiftly along. The regular dip of the oars, the distant song of the sailor, and sometimes the voice of a belated traveller at the ferry of Carrigaloe, alone broke the quietness of the land and sea and sky. The tide was in their favour, and in a few minutes Robin and his gossip rested on their oars under the dark shadow of the Giant's Stairs. Robin looked anxiously for the entrance to the Giant's palace, which, it was said, may be found by any one seeking it at midnight; but no such entrance could he see. His impatience had hurried him there before that time, and after waiting a considerable space in a state of suspense not to be described, Robin, with pure vexation, could not help exclaiming to his companion, " 'Tis a pair of fools we are, Tom Clancey, for coming here at all on the strength of a dream."

"And whose doing is it," said Tom, "but your own?"

At the moment he spoke they perceived a faint glimmering of

light to proceed from the cliff, which gradually increased until a porch big enough for a king's palace unfolded itself almost on a level with the water. They pulled the skiff towards the opening, and Robin Kelly, seizing his plough-iron, boldly entered with a strong hand and a stout heart. Wild and strange was that entrance, the whole of which appeared formed of grim and grotesque faces, blending so strangely each with the other that it was impossible to define any: the chin of one formed the nose of another; what appeared to be a fixed and stern eye, if dwelt upon, changed to a gaping mouth; and the lines of the lofty forehead grew into a majestic and flowing beard.

The more Robin allowed himself to contemplate the forms around him, the more terrific they became; and the stony expression of this crowd of faces assumed a savage ferocity as his imagination converted feature after feature into a different shape and character. Losing the twilight in which these indefinite forms were visible, he advanced through a dark and devious passage, whilst a deep and rumbling noise sounded as if the rock was about to close upon him, and swallow him up alive for ever. Now, indeed, poor Robin felt afraid.

"Robin, Robin," said he, "if you were a fool for coming here, what in the name of fortune are you now?" But, as before, he had scarcely spoken, when he saw a small light twinkling through the darkness of the distance, like a star in the midnight sky. To retreat was out of the question; for so many turnings and windings were in the passage, that he considered he had but little chance of making his way back. He, therefore, proceeded towards the bit of light, and came at last into a spacious chamber, from the roof of which hung the solitary lamp that had guided him.

Emerging from such profound gloom the single lamp afforded Robin abundant light to discover several gigantic figures seated round a massive stone table, as if in serious deliberation, but no word disturbed the breathless silence which prevailed. At the head of this table sat Mahon MacMahon himself, whose majestic beard had taken root, and in the course of ages grown into the stone slab. He was the first who perceived Robin; and instantly starting up, drew his long beard from out the huge piece of rock in such haste and with so sudden a jerk that it was shattered into a thousand pieces.

"What seek you?"' he demanded in a voice of thunder.

"I come," answered Robin, with as much boldness as he could put on, for his heart was almost fainting within him; "I come," said he, "to claim Philip Ronayne, whose time of service is out this night."

"And who sent you here?" said the giant.

" 'Twas of my own accord I came," said Robin.

"Then you must single him out from among my pages," said the giant; "and if you fix on the wrong one, your life is forfeit. Follow me." He led Robin into a hall of vast extent and filled with lights; along either side of which were rows of beautiful children, all apparently seven years old, and none beyond that age, dressed in green, and every one exactly dressed alike.

"Here," said Mahon, "you are free to take Philip Ronayne,

if you will; but, remember, I give you but one choice."

Robin was sadly perplexed; for there were hundreds upon hundreds of children; and he had no very clear recollection of the boy he sought. But he walked along the hall, by the side of Mahon, as if nothing was the matter, although his great iron dress clanked fearfully at every step, sounding louder than Robin's own sledge battering on his anvil.

They had nearly reached the end without speaking, when Robin, seeing that the only means he had was to make friends with the giant, determined to try what effect a few soft words might have.

" 'Tis a fine wholesome appearance the poor children carry," remarked Robin, "although they have been here so long shut out from the fresh air and the blessed light of heaven. 'Tis tenderly your honour must have reared them!"

"Aye," said the giant, "that is true for you; so give me your hand; for you are, I believe, a very honest fellow for a blacksmith."

Robin at the first look did not much like the huge size of the hand, and, therefore, presented his plough-iron, which the giant seizing, twisted in his grasp round and round again as if it had been a potato stalk. On seeing this all the children set up a shout of laughter. In the midst of their mirth Robin thought he heard his name called; and all ear and eye, he put his hand on the boy who he fancied had spoken, crying out at the same time, "Let me live or die for it, but this is young Phil Ronayne."

"It is Philip Ronayne —happy Philip Ronayne," said his young companions; and in an instant the hall became dark. Crashing noises were heard, and all was in strange confusion; but Robin held fast his prize, and· found himself lying in the grey dawn of the morning at the head of the Giant's Stairs with the boy clasped in his arms.

Robin had plenty of gossips to spread the story of his wonderful adventure: Passage, Monkstown, Carrigaline – the whole barony of Kerricurrihy rang with it.

"Are you quite sure, Robin, it is young Phil Ronayne you have brought back with you?" was the regular question; for although the boy had been seven years away, his appearance now was just the same as on the day he was missed. He had neither grown taller nor older in look, and he spoke of things which had happened before he was carried off as one awakened from sleep, or as if they had occurred yesterday.

"Am I sure? Well, that's a queer question," was Robin's reply; "seeing the boy has the blue eye of the mother, with the foxy hair of the father; to say nothing of the *purty* wart on the right side of his little nose."

However Robin Kelly may have been questioned, the worthy couple of Ronayne's Court doubted not that he was the deliverer of their child from the power of the giant MacMahon; and the reward they bestowed on him equalled their gratitude.

Philip Ronayne lived to be an old man; and he was remarkable to the day of his death for his skill in working brass and iron, which it was believed he had learned during his seven years' apprenticeship to the giant Mahon MacMahon.

19: THE ENCHANTMENT OF
EARL GERALD

In old times in Ireland there was a great man of the Fitzgeralds. The name on him was Gerald, but the Irish, that always had a great liking for the family, called him *Gearoidh Iarla* (Earl Gerald). He had a great castle or rath at *Mullymast* (Mullaghmast); and whenever the English Government were striving to put some wrong on the country, he was always the man that stood up for it. Along with being a great leader in a fight, and very skilful at all weapons, he was deep in the *black art,* and could change himself into whatever shape he pleased. His lady knew that he had this power, and often asked him to let her into some of his secrets, but he never would gratify her.

She wanted particularly to see him in some strange shape, but he put her off and off on one pretence or other. But she wouldn't be a woman if she hadn't perseverance; and so at last he let her know that if she took the least fright while he'd be out of his natural form, he would never recover it till many generations of men would be under the mould. "Oh! she wouldn't be a fit wife for Geariudh Iarla if she could be easily frightened. Let him but gratify her in this whim, and he'd see what a hero she was!" So one beautiful summer evening, as they were sitting in their grand drawing-room, he turned his face from her and muttered some words, and while you'd wink he was clever and clean out of sight, and a lovely *goldfinch* was flying about the room.

The lady, as courageous as she thought herself, was a little startled, but she held her own pretty well, especially when he came and perched on her shoulder, and shook his wings, and put his little beak to her lips, and whistled the delightfullest tune you ever heard. Well, he flew in circles round the room, and played *hide and go seek* with his lady, and flew out into the garden, and flew back again, and lay down in her lap as if he was asleep, and jumped up again.

Well, when the thing had lasted long enough to satisfy both, he took one flight more into the open air; but by my word he was soon on his return. He flew right into his lady's bosom, and the next moment a fierce hawk was after him. The wife gave one loud scream, though there was no need, for the wild bird came in like an arrow, and struck against a table with such force that the life was dashed out of him. She turned her eyes from his quivering body to where she saw the goldfinch an instant before, but neither goldfinch nor Earl Gerald did she ever lay eyes on again.

Once every seven years the Earl rides round the Curragh of Kildare on a steed, whose silver shoes were half an inch thick the time he disappeared; and when these shoes are worn as thin as a cat's ear he will be restored to the society of living men, fight a great battle with the English, and reign king of Ireland for two-score years.*

Himself and his warriors are now sleeping in a long cavern under the Rath of Mullaghmast. There is a table running along through the middle of the cave. The Earl is sitting at the head, and his troopers down along in complete armour both sides of the table, and their heads resting on it. Their horses, saddled and bridled, are standing behind their masters in their stalls at each side; and when the day comes, the miller's son that's to be born with six fingers on each hand, will blow his trumpet, and the horses will stamp and whinny, and the knights awake and mount their steeds,

---

*The last time *Gearoidh Iarla* appeared the horse-shoes were as thin as a sixpence.

and go forth to battle.

Some night that happens once in every seven years, while the Earl is riding round the Curragh, the entrance may be seen by anyone chancing to pass by. About a hundred years ago, a horse-dealer that was late abroad and a little drunk, saw the lighted cavern, and went in. The lights, and the stillness, and the sight of the men in armour, cowed him a good deal, and he became sober. His hands began to tremble, and he let a bridle fall on the pavement. The sound of the bit echoed through the long cave, and one of the warriors that was next him lifted his head a little, and said, in a deep hoarse voice, "Is it time yet?" He had the wit to say, "Not yet, but soon will," and the heavy helmet sank down on the table. The horse-dealer made the best of his way out, and I never heard of any other one having got the same opportunity.

20: THE STORY OF THE LITTLE BIRD

Many years ago there was a very religious and holy man, one of the monks of a convent, and he was one day kneeling at his prayers in the garden of his monastery, when he heard a little bird singing in one of the rose trees of the garden, and there never was anything that he heard in the world so sweet as the song of that little bird.

And the holy man rose up from his knees where he was kneeling at his prayers to listen to its song; for he thought he never in all his life heard anything so heavenly.

And the little bird, after singing for some time longer in the rose tree, flew away to a grove at some distance from the monastery, and the holy man followed it to listen to its singing, for he felt as if he could never be tired of listening to the sweet song that it was singing out of its throat.

And the little bird after that went away to another distant tree, and sung there for a while, and then to another tree, and so on in the same manner, but ever farther and farther away from the monastery, and the holy man still following it farther, and farther, and farther still listening delighted to its enchanting song.

But at last he was obliged to give up, as it was growing late in the day, and he returned to the convent, and as he approached it in the evening, the sun was setting in the west with all the most heavenly colours that were ever seen in the world, and when he came into the convent, it was nightfall.

And he was quite surprised at everything he saw, for they were all strange faces about him in the monastery that he had never seen before, and the very place itself, and everything about it, seemed to be strangely altered; and, altogether, it seemed entirely different from what it was when he left in the morning; and the garden was not like the garden where he had been kneeling at his devotion when he first heard the singing of the little bird.

And while he was wondering at all he saw, one of the monks of the convent came up to him, and the holy man questioned him, "Brother, what is the cause of all these strange changes that have taken place here since the morning?"

And the monk that he spoke to seemed to wonder greatly at his question, and asked him what he meant by the changes since morning? for, sure, there was no change; that all was just as before. And then he said, "Brother, why do you ask these strange questions, and what is your name? for you wear the habit of our order, though we have never seen you before."

So upon this the holy man told his name, and said that he had been at mass in the chapel in the morning before he had wandered away from the garden listening to the song of a little bird that was singing among the rose trees, near where he was kneeling at his prayers.

And the brother, while he was speaking, gazed at him very earnestly, and then told him that there was in the convent a tradition of a brother of his name, who had left it two hundred years before, but that what had become of him was never known.

And while he was speaking, the holy man said, "My hour of death is come; blessed be the name of the Lord for all his mercies to me, through the merits of his only-begotten Son."

And he kneeled down that very moment, and said, "Brother, take my confession, and give me absolution, for my soul is

departing."

And he made his confession, and received his absolution, and was anointed, and before midnight he died.

The little bird, you see, was an angel, one of the cherubim or seraphim; and that was the way that the Almighty was pleased in His mercy to take to Himself the soul of that holy man.

Notes on the Stories

1: THE STOLEN CHILD

This haunting poem first appeared in the *Irish Monthly* in December 1886. It marked Yeats's crucial decision to confine his poetry to Irish subjects. Its dreamy late-Romantic atmosphere is not typical of the folk belief in fairy changelings on which it draws, reflecting instead Yeats's own misty concept of the 'celtic twilight'. In a review of Lady Wilde's *Ancient Cures, Charms and Usages of Ireland* in 1890, he announced that 'the grey morning melancholy runs through all the legends of my people' – a view he must have been caused to revise on his later expeditions collecting folklore with Lady Gregory. Real folklore is more down-to-earth and robust than this; but the unearthly fragile elegance of 'The Stolen Child' has made it deservedly one of the most popular of Yeats's early poems. Yeats noted, 'The places mentioned are round about Sligo. Further Rosses is a very noted fairy locality. There is here a little point of rocks where, if anyone falls asleep, there is danger of their waking silly, the fairies having carried off their souls.'

2: THE PRIEST'S SUPPER

This sprightly legend is from the first major collection of Irish folklore, Thomas Crofton Croker's *Fairy Legends and Traditions of the South of Ireland* (1825–1828). Croker was a senior clerk in the Admiralty in London who gathered stories and traditions on walking tours in southern Ireland, and also begged stories from like-minded friends such as Thomas Keightley, author of *The Fairy Mythology*. Croker's first volume, which included 'The Priest's Supper', 'The Legend of Knockgrafton', 'Master and Man' and 'Daniel O'Rourke', was almost immediately translated into German by the Brothers Grimm, who saw its importance. Croker returned the compliment by translating the Grimms' long introductory essay in his third and final volume, which he dedicated to them. Although there is truth in Thomas Keightley's disgruntled comment that, 'some of the more amusing traits which (the Grimms) give as characteristic of the Irish fairies, owe their origin to the fancy of the writers, who were, in many cases, more anxious to produce amusing tales than to transmit legends faithfully', Croker's work was a confident and encouraging start to folklore collecting in Ireland, presenting the stories for the most part 'in the style in which they are generally related by those who believe in them'. Yeats originally planned simply to produce a new edition of Croker, before settling on the wider scope of his *Fairy and Folk Tales,* and Croker remained a chief source for his work. As with most folk tales and legends, 'The Priest's Supper' can be paralleled with similar stories told in many countries, as well as other Irish versions. Folklorists label such stories 'The Fairies' Prospect of Salvation'.

3: THE LEGEND OF KNOCKGRAFTON

This wide-spread legend is also from Croker's *Fairy Legends and Traditions*. Croker gives a tune for the fairies' song, 'commonly sung by every skilful narrator of the tale'. The fairies' words mean 'Monday, Tuesday', which Lusmore caps with 'and Wednesday', and Jack Madden ruins with 'and Thursday and Friday'. Croker notes that, 'In different parts of the country, of course various raths and mounds are assigned as the scene of fairy revelry. The writer's reason for selecting the moat of Knockgrafton was his having been told the legend within view of the place in August 1816, and with little variation from the words of the text.' A 'moat' is a tumulus or barrow; that of Knockgrafton is in Munster. Similar tales are told in many countries, but this type, known as 'The Gifts of the Little People', seems particularly popular in Ireland and in Japan, where it is used to point a moral to children. See the story 'The Old Man Who Had Wens' in Keigo Seki *Folktales of Japan* (1963).

4: A DONEGAL FAIRY

From Letitia McClintock 'Folk Lore of the County Donegal', *Dublin University Magazine* vol. 89, 1877. The 'Noman' motif, familiar from *The Odyssey* is found in many folk literatures. This version is unusual in that it avoids the joke that the human who has harmed the fairy or ogre gives their name as 'My ainsel' or some such, so that when the injured party is asked who hurt them, they can only say 'Myself'. Instead the story is used to point the moral that 'the gentry' will avenge all ill-treatment, and so must be treated with respect. Letitia McClintock collected many Ulster traditions but published only a few articles. She gives the narrator of 'A Donegal Fairy' as 'old Matt Craig', but this is probably a made-up name. It is typical of Yeats's small alterations to his sources that he amends her stage-Irish 'crathurs' to 'creatures'.

5: JAMIE FREEL AND THE YOUNG LADY

Also from Letitia McClintock 'Folk Lore of the County Donegal'. There are several Irish parallels, of which the closest is the story of 'Guleesh' collected by Douglas Hyde and translated in his *Beside the Fire* (1890). A recent retelling is N. Philip *Guleesh and the King of France's Daughter* (1986), illustrated with Victorian magic lantern slides by H. M. J. Underhill.

6: A LEGEND OF KNOCKMANY

This story, first printed in *Chambers's Journal*, is taken from William Carleton's *Tales and Sketches illustrating the Character, Usages, Traditions, Sports and Pastimes of the Irish Peasantry* (1845). Incorporating various devices known to folklorists as 'Tales of the Stupid Ogre', it is a skit on two of the great heroes of Irish story-telling, Finn and Cuchulain. Another version, 'Fion MacCuil and the Scotch

Giant', is in Patrick Kennedy's *Legendary Fictions of the Irish Celts* (1866). The tale first appeared in print in 1834, in Captain Marryat's seafaring novel *Peter Simple*, in which the master's mate O'Brien tells Peter 'how Fingal bothered the great Scotch giant'.

7: THE TWELVE WILD GEESE

With 'The Twelve Wild Geese' we enter the world of the international wonder tale. This type is known as 'The Maiden Who Seeks her Brothers'; the Grimms' version is called 'The Six Swans'. The story comes from *The Fireside Stories of Ireland* (1870) by the Dublin bookseller Patrick Kennedy, who published several excellent collections of stories he remembered from his childhood in County Wexford. These stories were told in English, though they are clearly derived from the Gaelic storytelling tradition. 'Bog-down', from which the shirts have to be made, is cotton-grass. There is another excellent Irish version, 'The Twelve Brothers', in Séamus Ó Duilearga *Seán Ó Conaill's Book* (tr. Maire MacNeill, 1981), a marvellous collection which gives the entire repertoire of a master storyteller.

8: THE LAZY BEAUTY AND HER AUNTS

'Lazy Beauty' is another of Patrick Kennedy's *Fireside Tales*. It is a version of the international tale known as 'The Three Old Women Helpers', which is itself essentially a variant of the 'Rumpelstiltskin' type.

9: THE HAUGHTY PRINCESS

This third story from Kennedy's *Fireside Tales* is a version of the tale type known to scholars by the title of the Grimms' story, 'King Thrushbeard'.

10: FAR DARRIG IN DONEGAL

Yeats gave his own title to this story from Letitia McClintock's 'Folk Lore of the County Donegal', associating the 'big man' of the story with the supernatural being known as the Far Darrig (*Fear Dearg*, red man), whom he describes as 'the practical joker of the other world'. Yeats himself recorded a rather inferior version of this tale from a Sligo man named Michael Hart, and published it as 'A Fairy Enchantment' in *Irish Fairy Tales* and with variations elsewhere. The tale of 'The Man Who Had No Story' is common in Ireland and Scotland, and seems to be peculiar to the Gaelic tradition.

11: DONALD AND HIS NEIGHBOURS

From a rare early nineteenth-century chapbook, the *Royal Hibernian Tales*. Yeats could not find a copy of this, so his friend AE (the poet and mystic George Russell) copied it out for him in Dublin. It has now been reprinted in *Béaloideas*, the Journal of the Folklore of Ireland Society, vol. 10, 1940. The *Royal Hibernian Tales* are mentioned by William Makepeace Thackeray in his *Irish Sketchbook* (1842), in which he too printed the story of 'Donald and his Neighbours'. The story is a version of the type internationally known as 'The Rich and the Poor Peasant'. Henry Glassie's excellent anthology *Irish Folktales* (1985) contains a version of this story, 'Huddon and Duddon and Donald O'Leary' tape-recorded from the Fermanagh storyteller Hugh Nolan in 1972 which is of particular interest as Mr Nolan evidently learned the story from a reprint of the *Royal Hibernian Tales* text. His version shows what a gifted storyteller's creative involvement with his material can mean, while still remaining faithful to the original.

12: Master and Man

From T. Crofton Croker *Fairy Legends and Traditions*. Croker was told many stories of men obliged to keep company with the fairies, 'going far and near with them, day and night – to London one night and to America the next; and the only horses they made use of for these great journeys were cabbage stumps in the form of natural horses.' Sean O'Sullivan's *Folktales of Ireland* (1966) has a splendid tale. 'Seán Palmer's Voyage to America with the Fairies', in which the journey is taken in a fairy boat, and the contented Seán draws the cheerful moral, 'a lucky man only needs to be born'. The Rinka *(rinceadh)* is an Irish dance.

13: The Witches' Excursion

From Patrick Kennedy *Legendary Fictions of the Irish Celts* (1866). This legend, like 'Master and Man' and 'Jamie Freel' makes use of the common motif of the ride with the fairies, this time transferred to witches. Among many versions of this in British legend, one might mention the story of the Laird of Duffus, given in Sir Walter Scott's *Minstrelsy of the Scottish Border:* he was whirled to the King of France's cellar when he repeated the fairies' cry of 'Horse and Hattock', and found there drunk by the king's butler the following morning.

14: The Man Who Never Knew Fear

Collected and translated by Douglas Hyde, this tale is internationally known as 'The Youth Who Wanted to Know what Fear Is'. It is common in Ireland.

15: The Horned Women

From Lady Jane Francesca Wilde *Ancient Legends, Mystic charms, and Superstitions of Ireland* (1887). A number of legends incorporate this 'your house is on fire' ruse for getting rid of unwelcome fairy guests, with its reminiscence of the children's rhyme of 'Ladybird, ladybird, fly away home', but the eerie horns of the witches are unique to this powerful legend of Lady Wilde's. Lady Wilde and her husband

Sir William, parents of the playwright Oscar Wilde, were notably eccentric figures in nineteenth-century Dublin. Some of their own actions and words have passed into folklore: Lady Wilde is particularly remembered for her rebuke to a slatternly maid, 'Why do you put the plates on the coal scuttle? What are the chairs meant for?' Sir William was a doctor who accepted payment in folklore from his poorer patients, publishing a volume on *Irish Popular Superstitions* (1853). Lady Wilde, who also published political verse as 'Speranza', gathered her husband's collections into two fascinating if unreliable rag-bags of books, *Ancient Legends* and its sequel, *Ancient Cures, Charms and Usages in Ireland (1890)*.

16: DANIEL O'ROURKE

From Croker *Fairy Legends and Traditions*. Croker compares Daniel O'Rourke to Astolpho, who travels to the moon in Ariosto's epic sixteenth-century poem *Orlando Furioso*, and says that the tale 'is a very common one, and is here related according to the most authentic version'. Folklorists list such stories under the title, 'The Man Carried Through the Air by Geese'.

17: THE SOUL CAGES

From Croker *Fairy Legends and Traditions*. The notion of the soul cages is most poetic and intriguing, but is not confined to Ireland; as Croker noted, the Grimms had collected a similar legend in Germany, translated by Donald Ward as 'The Merman and the Farmer' in *The German Legends of the Brothers Grimm* (1981).

18: THE GIANT'S STAIRS

From Croker *Fairy Legends and Traditions*. This and the following story both conform to the widespread legend type known as 'The Seven Sleepers'.

19: THE ENCHANTMENT OF EARL GERALD

From Patrick Kennedy *Legendary Fictions of the Irish Celts*. Kennedy says that 'What we heard from Mrs K. (his grandmother) in 1816, or thereabouts, is here given to the reader most conscientiously.'

20: THE STORY OF THE LITTLE BIRD

Contributed by T. Crofton Croker to *The Amulet, or Christian and Literary Remembrancer* for 1827, edited by S. C. Hall. Croker explains that on a recent trip to the south of Ireland collecting 'legendary tales' he often found people willing to share stories at the religious assemblies known as 'patterns' held at the holy well dedicated to a patron saint. At such meetings, 'legends of all descriptions, but more particularly legends of saints, are told more freely than under other circumstances'. He describes the scene: 'It was a beautiful summer's evening, and, weary with walking, I had sat down to rest upon a grassy bank, close to a holy well. I felt refreshed at the sight of the clear cold water, through which pebbles glistened, and sparks of silvery air shot upwards: in short, I was in the temper to be pleased. An old woman had concluded her prayers, and was about to depart, when I entered into conversation with her, and I have written the very words in which she related to me the legend of the Song of the Little Bird.' This legend is again internationally known, as 'The Monk and the Bird', but it is perhaps particularly at home in Ireland. Sean O'Sullivan prints another version in his *Legends from Ireland*. and rightly remarks that the monk's sudden ageing recalls the fate of the hero Oisín when he returns to Ireland from the Land of Youth. It also brings to mind the little verse scribbled in the margin of a manuscript by an unknown Irish monk of the eighth or ninth century, translated by Kenneth Hurlstone Jackson in his *Celtic Miscellany*: 'The little bird has given a whistle from the tip of its bright yellow beak; the blackbird from the yellow-topped bough sends forth its call over Loch Loígh.'

W B. Yeats's writings on folk and fairy lore can mostly be found in the two collections of tales from which this volume has been drawn, in *The Celtic Twilight* (now included in the volume *Miscellanies*), in Lady Gregory's *Visions and Beliefs in the West of Ireland* (2nd edition, 1970), and in the two volumes of his *Uncollected Prose* (ed. John P. Frayne and Colton Johnson, 1975). The first volume of his *Collected Letters* (ed. John Kelly and Eric Domville, 1986) covers the period (1865-1895) of his most intense interest in folklore.

Folklorists can find their way about the Irish material by using three technical guides, *A Bibliography of Irish Ethnology and Folk Tradition* by Caoimhín Ó Danachair (1978), *A Handbook of Irish Folklore* by Seán Ó Súilleabháin and *The Types of the Irish Folktale* by Seán Ó Súilleabháin and Reidar Th. Christiansen (1967).